For my grandfather, Derek Rover Humphrey – KH

For Frankie and Minnie, my two little Whisperers – CC

STRIPES PUBLISHING
An imprint of Little Tiger Press
1 The Coda Centre, 189 Munster Road,
London SW6 6AW

A paperback original
First published in Great Britain in 2015
Text copyright © Kris Humphrey, 2015
Illustration copyright © Chellie Carroll, 2015

ISBN: 978-1-84715-605-1

Printed and bound in the UK.

10 9 8 7 6 5 4 3 2 1

WARNING CRY

Kris Humphrey

Illustrated by Chellie Carroll

Stripes

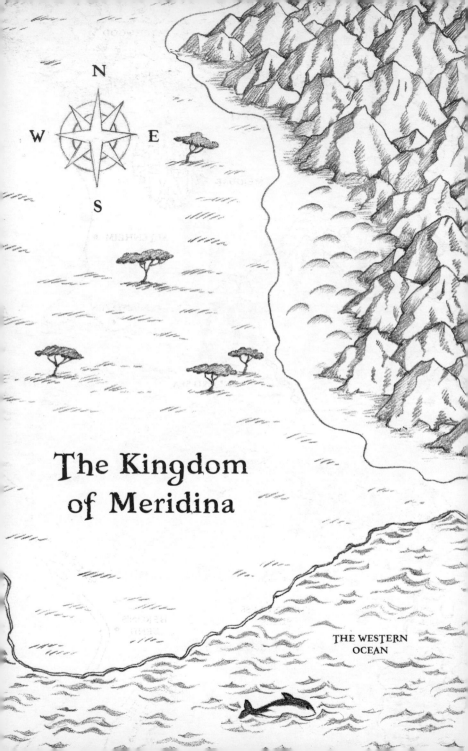

CHAPTER 1

The sun rose behind Sleeping Rock and, as its rays crested the summit, long shafts of light burst across the savannah: pink, orange, brilliant white. The earth woke, insects buzzed into the air and the acacia trees shifted in the breeze.

Nara stood at the front of the house, her pack, bow and arrows beside her and her water skin hitched to her belt. She would miss this sight. Sleeping Rock would always mean home to her, no matter how glad she was to be leaving.

She could hear her father in the kitchen, cleaning up after breakfast. Her mother was tending to the cows, milking them in her quick, orderly way, and Nara's sister, Kali, was busy cleaning out the chicken sheds and collecting eggs to sell at the next market.

All this hard work going on around her felt like a reproach.

Nara was a Whisperer, not a farmer. She had been chosen on the day she was born, when a single white feather landed at the door of her parents' home.

Everybody knew that Whisperers were vital to the kingdom of Meridina, that they were healers and channelers of the earth's power, and that they had saved the kingdom from destruction in the past. But still Nara's parents had cursed the arrival of the white feather, along with the raven who delivered it.

What use were a Whisperer's skills when only hard work and experience could put food on the table?

Nara was a good Whisperer – she could heal, she could communicate with almost any kind of animal and she could set protective wards that kept predators at bay. But her daily training took her away from the family farm and, at the age of twelve, she still couldn't milk a cow properly, or separate a herd for market, or plant maize that would grow in the crumbly red soil of their farmland.

Although her parents never said so, Nara knew she was a disappointment to them. It was clear in the way they constantly praised her sister. Kali was devoted to the farm in a way that Nara never could be.

And now the raven had visited their home once again.

It had come like a falling shadow, bringing Nara an urgent message from the palace in Meridar. She had closed her eyes and the raven had placed images in her mind. She saw a strange, dense forest – more green than she could ever have imagined. And between the trees she had seen the Narlaw, the shape-shifting demons she had learned so much about in her Whisperer training. In the raven's vision they took the forms of women, men and wolves, and Nara had felt a terrible chill run through her. A hundred years had passed since these demons were last banished into the Darklands. But the raven's message was clear: the Narlaw had returned and Nara, along with all of the Whisperers of Meridina, must journey to the palace for a council of war.

Despite her anxiety, Nara had needed no further convincing to leave. She had packed her things and, one day later, she was ready for the journey north.

She watched the morning light creep over the clefts and ridges of Sleeping Rock. Behind her, on the far side of the house, the cattle lowed and snorted in their pens – those great grey cows whose bristly chins Nara had always loved to stroke.

Today she would leave all this behind. Her parents didn't understand the responsibility of a Whisperer – that Nara had been born to protect the wilds, and that the Narlaw were the biggest threat they faced. But she was determined to show her family who she really was, to go from healer to warrior and banish the demons just like Queen Amina had a hundred years ago. She felt a ripple of fear at the thought. She had learned the theory of banishment from Lucille, her mentor, but to be faced with a real shape-shifting demon was a different matter all together. They were stronger than three men combined and they could steal your form and drop you into an endless, dreamless sleep at a single touch…

Nara gripped her bow tightly and breathed the cool air. She reached out with her Whisperer sense and felt the world around her – the sway of the grass, the bush larks darting overhead. All of this would be gone if the Narlaw were allowed to return. The demons lived only to destroy, feeding on the living parts of the world as a fire feeds on dry timber.

Her journey would span the length of Meridina, up into the cold north of the kingdom, a place that was completely unknown to her. To where the ravens roosted and the Darklands sat just beyond the mountains, threatening.

Paws padded lightly on the earth behind her, reminding Nara that she wouldn't be facing these challenges alone. She turned as her leopard companion, Flame, emerged from the house.

Some things are worth rising early for, Flame said.

Her words rang out in Nara's mind and she felt comforted as Flame came to her side. The bond they shared and their silent way of whispering together were the greatest gifts Nara posessed. To other people it seemed strange and unsettling, but to Nara and Flame it was utterly natural.

Do you think they have mornings like this in the north? whispered Nara.

Flame squinted into the sunrise and flicked her long black-tipped tail.

Not like this, she said.

Nara lay her hand on the soft patterned fur of her companion's back. Flame was slender and proud, the colour of the savannah itself.

A cool day, said Flame, flaring her nostrils.

There was a thinness to the air, the clouds gathering and shifting.

A good day for a long walk, Nara said.

Flame looked up, her sand-coloured eyes regarding Nara intently.

A long walk together, Flame said.

Always, said Nara, scratching Flame between the ears.

The sun had crested the long, bare summit of Sleeping Rock now and the savannah was bathed in light – the wide-spaced acacia and date trees, the tufts of red-grass and dropseed.

How cold do you think it is in Meridar? asked Nara.

Colder than we could imagine, said Flame, pacing a circle around Nara. *They say the sun only rises for a few hours a day at this time of year – that they have winters there, and snow.*

Well, I'm glad I packed my thickest blanket, said Nara. *Us furless creatures have to be careful.*

She had packed all the medicines and tools of her trade, too – the soft, small pouches full of herbs, root stalks and blends, the finger-length sickle with its bone handle and curved steel blade, fabric strips for bandaging, her tiny crucible and tinder.

Perhaps we should go, said Flame. *I don't think there's going to be a big farewell party.*

Nara ducked back inside the house and stepped quietly into the kitchen where her father stood with his back to the door.

"We're going," she said. "Would you say goodbye to Mother and Kali?"

Her father turned and looked at her with what seemed to be his usual impatient expression. But as Nara held his gaze, she realized there was sorrow in his eyes, too.

"You'll pass close to the Rift," he said, shifting his eyes down to his boots. "There are bands of nomads on the move there. Some farmers ran into them and their meeting wasn't friendly."

"I'll be careful," said Nara.

She knew of the nomads by their fierce reputation only. They were tribal people, herders of cattle and skilled hunters and warriors.

Nara stood awkwardly for a moment until, to her surprise, her father stepped forwards and gave her a quick, powerful hug. She breathed in his familiar scent, storing the memory away.

"You be safe," he told her.

Nara nodded.

She left without saying goodbye to Kali or her mother, fearing some kind of argument, or worse: the stony silence she so often received.

She walked with Flame into the savannah, glancing back again and again until her home had vanished in the distance, replaced by the grasslands, the trees and the endless sky.

They walked the whole morning without resting, through long swathes of grass and keeping to the dappled shade of the trees when they could.

Flame padded beside Nara, moving in a way that seemed lazy and alert all at once. Her ears twitched this way and that, seeking out and distinguishing all of the sounds of the grasslands around her. Nara loved to watch Flame move, the way her shoulders rolled, shifting the wonderful, black-crescent patterning of her fur.

You want to race? asked Nara. *Or are your leopard legs too tired?*

I could win with my legs tied together, said Flame. She peered sideways at Nara, her eyes glinting.

Nara grinned down at her. Then, without warning, she sprinted out in front. Sunlight flashed and the grass swept at her sandals as she ran with long, smooth strides. Her knee-length dress flapped against her legs in the breeze. She heard the rhythmic patter of Flame's paws behind her and, just as her companion caught up, Nara swerved to her right, slapped her palm on the fat trunk of an acacia tree and called, *I win!*

Flame arrived, shaking her head and panting.

Not a fair race, she said.

You never asked where we were racing to, said Nara.

And you wouldn't have told me.

Flame flopped to the ground, legs sprawling. Her markings matched the shade perfectly.

Come on, said Nara, smiling. *Don't be a bad loser.*

They set off once again, north-east towards the river towns. Nara's plan was to board a ferry or a fishing boat on the great Salesi River, to carry them north at least as far as the Inland Sea. By her guess there would be three days' walking before they reached the river. Beyond that she didn't know. No one she knew had ever crossed into the north, and Nara was certain that no Southlander had travelled there with a hunting cat by their side.

At midday they stopped to rest beneath a strangler-fig tree. Nara ate a few mouthfuls of the delicious salty cheese she had packed and one of the small flatbreads her father baked every morning. Flame stayed by her side, opting not to hunt. She could go for days without eating, which gave her a good excuse for the hours she spent lounging about.

Nara held out a handful of food. *You still like cheese, don't you?* she said. *You must be hungry by now.*

Flame peered at the food as if it were a lump of dung. *Thanks*, she said. *But I'll take my chances.*

Well, you're missing out, said Nara, chewing on one final piece before packing the rest away for later.

Flame stretched out and her white belly fur stuck out in irresistible tufts. Nara gave her a rub and Flame closed her eyes, letting out the soft, contented growl that was her version of a tame cat's purring.

Under a pink evening sky, Nara and Flame arrived in a shallow valley that was overlooked on one side by a long outcrop of bare granite. It was a perfect hunting ground, and Flame slinked off into the shadows while Nara trod the dusty valley in search of a place to sleep.

Soon she found a tall yellow fever tree with a thick, knotted trunk and a dense spread of branches. Casting out with her Whisperer sense, Nara found that the tree was not occupied, which was a relief – the last thing she wanted was to disturb a cobra or some other creature from its rest. She removed her sandals, tucking them into her pack, and began to climb.

Nara wound her way through the branches, savouring the feel of the smooth bark against her hands and feet. She found several outer branches grown together at the perfect angle for sleeping and removed her pack, tying it securely to an overhanging branch. This was where they would spend the night.

Nara reclined against the graceful curves of the tree and unrolled her blanket. She was exhausted, but excitement and fear ran together in her blood like a river after the rains.

By the time Flame returned from her hunt,

the sky was black and strewn with stars. Nara tracked her companion's approach all the way from the craggy edges of the outcrop, through the sparsely wooded valley and up, quick and effortless, into the fever tree. Flame was aglow with satisfaction and, as she curled up against Nara, her warmth was welcome.

Sleep lightly, Flame whispered as she settled down. *I'm not the only hunter in this valley tonight.*

Nara closed her eyes, but for a long time she was unable to relax, reaching out with her senses to scan the ground below.

Nara woke and found her legs cold beneath the blanket.

Flame was gone.

She peered into the dark, glancing about her and probing with her Whisperer sense. Only then did she find Flame, crouching flat against an upper branch, her ears stiffly angled at the ground.

Nara crawled up to join her.

Quiet, Flame whispered.

Nara followed her companion's gaze into the deep, textured shadows at the foot of the tree. She was suddenly aware of several creatures nearby. They pulsed with sharpness and hunger. Nara strained to see. There was a thick, wild scent on the air. She heard a snort of breath and the scuff of paws in the dust below.

Jackals. A pack of them.

They were a sandy brown colour with streaks of black and white across their backs, and they passed directly beneath the tree in a broad, unruly formation. These dogs were hunting and their tall ears twitched, alert for any sign of danger or prey. If they saw, heard or smelled Nara or Flame they would trap them there in the tree, waiting with infinite patience until starvation drove them down into their jaws.

Flame lay deathly still and Nara glanced past the slow-moving jackals to the nearby trees and the rocky hillside, seeking an escape route. But there was none.

She counted the dogs as they passed. There were sixteen of them, thin and battle-scarred. The very last of them paused beneath the fever tree.

Flame tensed, almost imperceptibly. For all her lazy habits she was a predator equal to any in the savannah. Nara glanced down to where her quiver and bow hung in the branches, hoping desperately that it wouldn't come to that.

The dog sniffed the ground at its feet and swung its head to either side, scanning the darkness.

Silently Nara rehearsed the still-ward she had learned from Lucille. Only once before had she tried it, on a crazed bull that had already been penned into a paddock by a group of farmers. But even if Nara captured this jackal in the still-ward, the rest of the pack would soon realize what had happened. There was nothing she or Flame could do against so many of them.

The dog scratched the dirt at the base of the tree and rubbed its neck against the bark. Nara watched it sniff the tree trunk. It would smell them there, surely. Her pulse accelerated and she felt Flame rise, ready to pounce.

But then, with a flick of its tail and its ears flat against its head, the animal trotted on into the bush.

Nara lay still, barely breathing, until she felt the band of jackals clear the valley and vanish out on to the plains.

CHAPTER 2

The second day of their journey began at dawn. After their encounter with the jackals, Nara had barely slept and her legs were heavy as she trod through the early morning light.

Flame, predictably, had settled quickly back to sleep and she now padded beside Nara with a freshness that Nara envied.

There are tracks everywhere, Flame said. *Hare, mongoose, impala. We must be close to the Rift. Maybe we should take a short cut through the hunting grounds?*

Nara frowned at the idea. *I think it's better if we stay on this path*, she said. *It's further to walk, but there are too many predators who hunt the Rift.*

Flame tilted her head in silent agreement, but Nara sensed her companion's disappointment.

You'll find mongoose in this valley, too, said Nara, *or you can have some of my cheese and bread.*

Bread is as tasteless as dirt, said Flame, shaking her head to emphasize her point. *You must have to swallow hard to keep that stuff in your stomach.*

Nara smiled. She wondered if all cats were as fussy about what they ate. *Well, anyway,* she said, *the Rift is too dangerous. I don't have your speed or your teeth, remember.*

Flame flicked her tail playfully. *I always forget how slow you two-legged creatures are.*

Nara laughed, but both she and Flame knew this was a serious point. The Rift was not a place to enter lightly. Its deep, rocky fissures held pools of rainwater that were havens for plant life. But they were also the haunts of the savannah's most dangerous creatures – snakes, buffalo, wild dogs and even lions sought food and shelter there.

And then there was the place's other name – Demons' Door. It was said that the earth's power grew thin in the Rift, that unnatural creatures could use it to force their way through into Meridina.

The path took them down an incline into a dry river bed. Bush larks whistled back and forth on the low ridge above the path. Nara glanced up, shielding her eyes from the sun. There was a subtle shifting in the shadows and the birds fell silent.

Nara felt her heartbeat quicken. Beside her, Flame dropped into a defensive, prowling posture and the bond between them pulsed with the leopard's alertness.

On the ridge, she whispered to Flame.

But she was too late. A rain of pebbles tumbled down the slope and a voice growled, low and threatening, behind them:

"Halt, Whisperer."

From the rocks emerged two women and a man. They were nomads of the plains, each wearing loose trousers and smocks of coarse fabric dyed in earthy, camouflaged colours. A variety of knives, small weapons and tools hung from the warriors on leather straps. Two of them carried bows, which were now aimed at Nara and Flame. The woman at the head of the pack held a short sword, its sharp tip pointing directly at Nara.

Flame bristled and snarled, and Nara reached for her own bow.

"Lower that arm," commanded the woman.

Nara slowly did so, staring into the woman's ash-streaked face. On one cheek was drawn an oval and on the other a lightning fork.

"A fine creature," the woman said. "I hope you have it well trained."

Nara didn't answer. She heard the bow strings creak as the two archers held their weapons taut. Nara probed the edges of the ravine with her Whisperer sense and felt the movement of others. They had walked into a trap and she cursed herself for not spotting it.

The woman with the sword whistled three times, mimicking the call of a bush lark, and three more nomad warriors stepped slowly into the river basin from the surrounding rocks and trees.

Flame snarled and prepared to pounce.

No! said Nara. *Please. They'll shoot us before you can do anything.*

Flame reluctantly obeyed – Nara could feel the effort her companion was making to keep her fighting instincts at bay.

A short, broad-shouldered man stepped to the forefront of the small group of nomads. "Thank you, Kalte," he said. "You may stand down."

The archers lowered their bows, but kept their eyes nervously on Flame. As the woman brought down her sword, Nara breathed again, though her every muscle remained tense.

"My apologies," said the leader. "But we can no longer be sure of a peaceful meeting when our peoples come together."

"Our peoples?" said Nara. She cast her gaze around the fierce, suspicious faces that surrounded them. Flame crouched by her side, ears flat against her skull, claws ready.

"Yes," said the man. "We are people of the Red Sands. Nomads, as you call us. And you are from the settlements. You say we hunt on your land, that we steal your cattle, and we say that no piece of land may be owned by anyone but the Earth Mother."

He smiled. "So, you see, we are different peoples."

Nara nodded. "We're simply travelling to the river," she said. "Our journey is urgent – we must go quickly."

"And we, too, have urgent matters to attend to," said the man, his smile fading into a grave expression. "Matters that would benefit from the craft of a Whisperer."

Nara glanced down at Flame.

We should run now, Flame said. *Lose them in the Rift.*

We wouldn't go three paces before an arrow cut us down, Nara whispered.

There were more than just two archers in the nomad group, and these people were lean and sharp-eyed, used to hunting prey and seeing off packs of predators in order to survive.

"Come," called the leader. "You have nothing to fear from us."

Nara searched his eyes for signs of untruth and the man watched her back. Her feet stood ready to run and the man sensed her indecision.

He raised a hand. "Please," he said. "In the name of the sun, we ask your help. Only that. We offer food and safety. You would be our guests."

I can sense no violence in him, Nara whispered to Flame. *But equally I think we have no choice.*

Flame flared her nostrils, flicking her tail in anger. *I should have heard them coming,* she said. *But you're right. What choice do we have?*

Nara met the leader's eyes and nodded once.

"Good," the man said, inclining his head. "Please. This way."

He led them from the path into a shallow ravine that had once been a river gully. The rest of the band fell in around them and Flame hissed at any who came too close. The sun blazed above the walls of the ravine and Nara walked with sweat on her brow, in and out of shadow. As she watched the tough, well-armed plains people, she wondered whether she and Flame were truly their guests … or their prisoners.

CHAPTER 3

Dawn listened to the rain as it gushed through the old stone guttering of the spiral tower. This was the third rainy day in a row and the yellow stone buildings of Meridar had turned a drab brown under the relentless autumn downpour. She found herself longing for her home in the Southlands once again, and not just because of this cursed northern weather. On the other side of the huge desk sat Lady Tremaine, the king's warden, and she was in a foul mood. Dawn had insisted that today's meeting take place in her own chambers and the warden was not happy about it.

She's still going, said Ebony, perched on the back of Dawn's carved wooden chair.

I doubt she'll ever stop, whispered Dawn.

"...and I shall repeat what I said earlier," droned the warden. "These chambers are not the place for an official meeting. To exclude the king is close to treason. I really do not see why palace protocol should be ignored in such a way."

The warden sat back in her chair, finally finished, glaring around the table with her arms folded.

Dawn glanced across at Captain Valderin, the Captain of the Palace Guard, and then at Magda, a senior lieutenant in the King's Guards of the Sun. Valderin wore a look of deep frustration. It appeared as though he was about to say something rash to the warden when Dawn cut in.

"I appreciate your patience, Lady Warden," she said. "But these chambers are more private than the official ones in the King's Keep. And, as we know, the king would rather not be disturbed by the unpleasant matters we discuss here."

The warden raised a dismissive eyebrow, but said no more on the subject. She knew very well that the king was falling further and further out of touch by the week, fixated on his daughter, the princess, and only attending to the most trifling matters of state.

Dawn took Lady Tremaine's silence as a begrudging agreement. Since Dawn had banished the Narlaw spy from the palace, Lady Tremaine had conceded gradually to Dawn's authority, though not by much, and not without complaint. The warden had even convinced the king that Dawn should be allowed to speak to Princess Ona. This had never been allowed before. King Eneron had completely shielded his daughter from the world of politics, and the wider world in general. Dawn only wished that Esther, her mentor and the previous Palace Whisperer, had been alive to see her progress.

"A week has passed since Ebony sent word out through the ravens," said Dawn. "We have three new Whisperers in the capital – not enough for a council of war, but the rest will come."

"We had better hope they do," said the warden.

"In the meantime," said Valderin, ignoring the warden's comment, "the Palace Guard and the Guards of the Sun have joined to create a combined defence force for the capital."

Magda nodded in agreement. "We've sent outriders to the neighbouring towns," she said, "with orders to be passed on. All local militia will send representatives to the palace for training. Meridina will have a standing army by the time the demons dare come out into the open."

"We'll need both soldiers and Whisperers to defeat the Narlaw," said Dawn. "Queen Amina's strength and the unity of the kingdom were the only things that saved Meridina a hundred years ago. We need the same. The demons have already attacked in the northern forests. They may not wait much longer to launch a full-scale invasion."

A grim silence followed. Only the rain could be heard, hammering against the stone on the veranda.

Ebony shifted uneasily on the back of Dawn's chair.

"If only we had a leader like Amina," said the warden. Her tone was wistful and falsely innocent – it was clearly meant as an insult to Dawn.

Dawn felt her cheeks colouring, but she swallowed the urge to reply. "Unity," she said at last, nodding at Valderin and Magda, who had done so well at working together already. "This is what we must strive for."

And I think we'll need a lot of luck, too, she whispered ruefully to Ebony.

Dawn rose from her seat, signalling that the meeting was over. She sensed again how young she was compared to those around her. The impossibility of her position weighed on her. How could a fifteen-year-old be expected to lead a nation into war?

Before Dawn could show the others out, a messenger rushed into the chamber. The look on his face was such that the news he carried could only be bad.

"Your pardon," said the messenger, red-faced and out of breath. "There's been a security breach – an intruder in Princess Ona's chambers."

Dawn shared a worried look with Valderin and immediately asked Ebony to fly on ahead of them. Then she rushed, with the guard captain and the lieutenant, out into the chilly stone corridors of the spiral tower.

As soon as Dawn arrived in Princess Ona's chambers, Ebony flapped across to meet her.

Narlaw, said Ebony. *I can sense it everywhere.*

Dawn scanned the lush furnishings of the reception room. Not much was out of place, but she too could feel the fading presence of a demon. A shudder ran up her spine.

Through here, said Ebony.

In Ona's dressing room the scene was very different. It had been ransacked – cupboards and dressers emptied out on to the floor, clothes everywhere and jewellery scattered across the top.

Ebony flew above the mess, then landed and began poking through the strings of pearls and fragile gold trinkets with her long curved beak.

Valderin stepped into the room behind Dawn. "What do you think?" he said.

"A demon was here," said Dawn. Saying it made her heart sink, but she should have known they'd be back. The question was: what did they want?

"Magda has gone to fetch Captain Niels of the

Guard of the Sun," said Valderin. "He should be able to tell us who was on guard duty here overnight. Perhaps we can determine when exactly they broke in and who might have seen them in the corridors. The king will be furious about this. We must make sure the princess is safe and find the demon as quickly as we can."

Dawn nodded. She looked to Ebony. *What do you see?*

The jewels carry the heaviest taint, said Ebony. *Do demons like shiny things?*

Perhaps this demon does, said Dawn.

She turned back to Captain Valderin, who was speaking quietly with a pair of Sun Guards, the two who had discovered the break-in.

"Where is the princess?" she asked them. "I must speak with her immediately."

Princess Ona had been taken to a separate wing and was under full guard. Magda was already there and Dawn asked whether she had managed to speak to

Captain Niels yet.

"Captain Niels gave me the guard roster from last night," said Magda. "He's with the king now, trying to reassure him that Ona is safe. This doesn't look good for the Guards of the Sun."

"A shape-shifter is hard to spot," said Dawn. "The king will understand."

Magda nodded, though they both knew the king was not an understanding man when it came to his daughter's safety.

Dawn thanked Magda and stepped past the guards into the princess's temporary quarters.

Ona rose from her cushioned chair as soon as she saw Dawn enter. Her worried look dissolved into a smile and she hurried to meet the Whisperer.

"It's terrible," said the princess. "Who would do such a thing? And to think, I was sleeping right there in the next room." She shook her head.

Dawn nodded in sympathy. "We'll find out what happened," she said. "But you're safe now. That's what really matters."

She peered over Ona's shoulder and saw Yusuf

among a group of young nobles who sat drinking tea. Yusuf nodded to her and she nodded back. He seemed to have recovered well following the ghost-sleep that he was put under when the Narlaw stole his form.

"I need to ask you some questions," said Dawn. "We have to know if anything was taken, or if you heard or saw anything out of the ordinary last night."

Ona stepped thoughtfully towards a window seat, away from her friends, and gestured for Dawn to sit beside her.

"I didn't hear a thing," said Ona. "That's what's frightening about it. How could someone do so much damage without making a sound?"

She stared out of the window at the grey sky and the rain.

Dawn kept silent – she didn't want to worry the princess.

"I haven't searched through everything yet," Ona continued, "so I don't know what was taken. Luckily I keep my most precious things in my bedchamber. No one could steal them without waking me."

"That's good," said Dawn. "Now, promise me

you'll do whatever Lieutenant Magda says, and that you'll tell me what's missing from your chambers as soon as you can?"

"Of course," said Ona. "If there's anything I can do to help you catch the intruder…" She paused. "You don't think it could be another…?"

A grave look passed across the princess' face. She glanced at Dawn and then out of the window into the neverending rain.

"Another Narlaw?" asked Dawn, softly.

"Yes," said Ona.

Dawn hesitated, but she realized that she couldn't keep it from Ona. "I think it was," she said, "which is why it's so important that we try to find out why it went through your belongings."

Ona nodded. "I'll go back right away and make an inventory." She spoke with determination, but Dawn could see that the princess was shaken.

Dawn rose and said goodbye, hearing the clink of tea cups and the idle chatter of the nobles resume as she left.

Walking back towards the spiral tower she

tried to guess what a demon would want with the contents of Ona's dressing room. The more she thought about it, the less sense it made. She was missing something. The Narlaw wouldn't go to such lengths unless they had a lot to gain.

Back in her chambers, all Dawn could do was wait until news came from Valderin or Magda or Ebony. She slid the leather-bound copy of the war diaries across her desk and began to read the words of the kingdom's greatest heroine, Queen Amina.

CHAPTER 4

The nomad camp was concealed by a thick grove of acacia trees in the shadow of a long, craggy hillside. Domed cowhide tents were placed haphazardly between the trees and cooking fires crackled, their smoke diffusing through the branches above.

Nara met the suspicious glances of the tribespeople as she passed. To them she was not just a Whisperer, but a farm girl, too – someone not to be trusted. It seemed foolish and unfair, but Nara thought of her parents and all the other farmers who believed the same thing about the nomads.

Flame prowled alongside Nara, ears twitching, tail low to the ground. *It's as if they've never seen a leopard before*, she said.

Well, whispered Nara. *Never one like you.*

They were led towards the centre of the camp where a large straight-sided tent stood between a pair of tall trees. There was an obvious tension in the camp. These people looked scared, and it made her wonder, more and more, what reason the leader of the tribe had for taking her and Flame as his "guests".

The leader raised the tent flap and ducked inside. Nara paused as one of the nomads held the entrance open for her. She knew nothing about these people. They had claimed to mean no harm, but could she trust them to keep their word?

What do you think? Nara asked Flame.

Flame peered into the dark of the tent, flexing her nostrils. *It smells like a home,* she said. *That's all. Their leader – there's no scent of fear or anger on him. Perhaps he's honest, but...*

Nara felt a hand against her back.

"Why have you stopped?" It was the scowling woman with the short sword.

Nara turned to face her and was about to reply when something else caught her attention.

Some distance away at the edge of the camp there was a presence, burning brightly. Nara glanced across, past the tents and the cooking fires and the pack animals.

A girl of about her own age, with her hair shaved close to her scalp, crept out of the bush. She was hurrying back into the camp, but before she had gone three paces she stopped and her head swung immediately in Nara's direction.

Nara met her gaze. That presence, it was unmistakeable. The girl was a Whisperer.

"Hey!" The woman prodded Nara, more roughly this time. "It's disrespectful to keep the Trailfinder waiting. Go inside. Now."

Nara stumbled forwards, stealing one last glance at the Whisperer girl before being propelled into the tribe leader's tent.

Flame snarled as she darted in beside Nara.

The nomads backed off, but one of the archers nocked an arrow and the woman who had pushed Nara drew her sword.

"Enough!" barked the tribe's leader. He stiffened

his thick neck and peered at the group with anger in his eyes. "Leave us," he ordered.

Nara watched the woman reluctantly lower her sword.

"I will stand guard, Trailfinder," she said.

"No," said the man. "You will leave." He turned his back on his scouts, pacing deeper into the tent.

Now Nara and Flame were alone with the Trailfinder. Nara scanned the tent, taking in the modest stacks of blankets and cushions, the woven baskets and the cold fire pit in the centre.

"You must excuse the quality of your welcome," said the man. "There is much fear among the plains people these days." He held out a hand in formal greeting. "I am Daan, Trailfinder of the Red Sands tribe."

Nara ignored his hand and simply nodded. "You claimed to need our help," she said. "We have a long way to travel, so please tell us what you want."

Flame stood poised at her side, eyes fixed on the leader.

Daan glanced nervously at her before replying.

"There are demons on the savannah," he said. "Shapeshifters that have taken the form of lions. They have attacked our herds and driven them away. Without cattle our tribe won't last another season."

He paused and Nara's heart sank as she realized what he was about to ask of her.

"You want us to banish these Narlaw," she said.

The silence stretched.

Finally, Daan nodded resignedly. "You're a Whisperer," he said. "Only you can help us."

"And what about the girl in your tribe?" asked Nara.

Daan narrowed his eyes, surprised, and, Nara thought, perhaps impressed.

"She was chosen by the raven, yes," he said, "but she cannot banish demons. Here we don't send our young girls away to be trained as Whisperers. We must keep the tribe together, especially those who are so skilled at hunting and tracking."

Nara could see how every person would be needed by the tribe, but she felt anger towards this man. How could he go against the wishes of the earth itself? How could he keep a young Whisperer from the life she was born to lead?

Daan seemed to sense her feeling. "We humbly request your help," he said, bowing his head.

Nara glanced at Flame. *If there are Narlaw here*, she whispered, *then we should do something. Without their cattle these people will starve.*

And if he's lying? said Flame.

Nara studied the stocky, sun-ravaged tribe-leader.

"It will not just be the Red Sands who are ruined by the demons," said Daan. "Soon enough they will attack the farms, the towns – your people will suffer as we do now."

He's right, we can't ignore this, said Nara.

What if you're wrong? said Flame, snorting. *What if this is some kind of trick? We'd be disobeying a direct order from the Palace Whisperer and we'll both be in serious trouble if we miss the council of war.*

But Nara had to act. Despite the summons, she couldn't leave these people to battle the Narlaw alone.

She looked at Daan. "We'll help you," she said, ignoring the spike of anger that she felt from Flame.

"But we can't stay long. We've been summoned to Meridar for a council of war."

Daan fixed her with a look of deep gratitude and began ushering them outside into the blinding daylight.

"You have my thanks," he said. "And the thanks of the whole tribe. You must have some food while we prepare a tracking party."

Nara was taken to a cooking fire and handed a plate of stew. The ash-streaked warriors of the Red Sands tribe moved around her and Flame, staring openly at this strange farm girl and her friend, the leopard.

Flame gnawed sulkily on a raw chunk of beef that had been cast at her feet.

At least the eating is good, she said.

But Nara had no appetite. She had hoped for more time before facing the Narlaw. She was expecting her first confrontation to come in the north, surrounded by other Whisperers, not here, alone, in the savannah.

It appeared she had been very wrong.

Nara and Flame left the camp as part of a small group of hunters. The sun blazed at its midday peak. There was no wind to ruffle the grass or the trees, only the relentless buzz and click of insects, as if the earth itself were agitated by the heat.

There were just six people in the hunting party, including Nara and Flame, and, much to Nara's dislike, the group was led by the scout with the short sword who had ordered her about like a prisoner. This woman's name was Kalte, the lightning symbol drawn in ash on her right cheek signifying that she was a warrior of the highest prestige.

Behind Kalte walked the girl Nara had spotted as she'd entered the camp – the Whisperer. Her name was Tuanne and she was Kalte's daughter. She had no companion that Nara could see, but was constantly glancing out into the bush.

Nara reached out once or twice and felt a shy, wary animal presence there. She strode alongside Flame, watching the girl as much as she watched the surrounding trees and grasses for signs of danger. This girl's very existence was fascinating to Nara – a Whisperer who had never been trained, who seemed to be keeping her companion hidden from the rest of the tribe. Nara couldn't imagine being separated from Flame in that way. Although she didn't know her at all, she felt sorry for Tuanne, and Nara's own family problems seemed much smaller all of a sudden.

The trail quickly drew them in the direction of the Rift. To Nara this was no surprise. It was such a secluded, sinister place.

We should have come this way to start with, Flame said, as they moved ever closer to the vast cliffs and gorges. *We would have avoided these people and been halfway to the river towns by now.*

And we would have run into the Narlaw on our own, said Nara. *They've taken the form of lions. At least now we are with people who know this place.*

Flame didn't answer and they continued along the path in silence.

Nara squinted at the cracked and foreboding

landscape ahead. Those cliffs and ravines were a haven for predators. And now they had been inhabited by the worst creatures of all. She had been told so much about the Narlaw that to be seeking them out in the flesh seemed unreal.

The moment they left the camp it was clear to Nara that her help was not needed in tracking. The nomads were true experts, studying the ground, tasting the wind and immediately spotting the tiniest signs that a creature had passed that way. Kalte strode ahead, tracking the movements of the Narlaw almost as quickly as Nara could walk.

When Nara spotted her first lion-print she gasped at its size and stopped in shock. She had never seen a lion, only ever sensed them out beyond the protective wards she placed around her family farm.

She felt Flame's soft fur brush against her hand and it brought her back to the present. Several of the hunters had stopped to stare at her, Tuanne included.

Come, said Flame. *We have warriors on our side now.*

Nara forced a smile and bent to adjust her sandal strap as if that was why she had stopped. She slid her hand across Flame's back and walked with the warmth of her companion against her palm.

She had wanted so badly to leave the stifling atmosphere of her home that she had failed to grasp the reality of what she was heading into. The pawprints they were following through the dust were real, made by demons in the most deadly form they could possibly have taken. Nara was flooded by doubt. Who was she to promise her services to the Red Sands tribe? She had never seen – let alone banished – a demon. She had been taught the theory, that by channelling the earth's power you could send a demon to the Darklands, leaving only a shadow of ash in this world. But could she really do that now? On her own?

Look, said Flame.

Nara peered off to the left of the trail. Most of the hunters had pushed ahead, leaving Nara and

Flame to catch up. But Tuanne had lagged behind, too, and she had strayed from the track, off into a patchy thicket of thorn bushes.

Nara shielded her eyes from the sun and saw a small, light-coloured shape rising on its hind legs in front of Tuanne. She saw the curl of a tail and twitching movements. Tuanne bent and held out her hand. The animal ate whatever was offered. The girl looked pleased, but tense. She clearly didn't know she was being watched.

What is it? asked Nara.

Flame squinted. *A monkey,* she said. *A red-back.*

I knew she was hiding a companion somewhere, said Nara.

She glanced ahead to where the rest of the band were. No one was watching so she ducked into the thorn thicket, closely followed by Flame.

Tuanne turned with a gasp. The monkey dropped on to all fours and bared a line of very sharp teeth. Her fur was mostly white, with a stripe of deep red running vertically up her spine. She hissed and danced anxiously around Tuanne's feet, finally clambering up on to her shoulder.

"Don't worry," said Nara. "I won't tell anyone."

Flame kept her distance. The red-back was small, but underestimating such a fierce little creature was a good way to receive a nasty bite.

"What do you want?" said Tuanne. "Did my mother send you to spy?"

"No," said Nara. "I saw you in the camp. If you're a Whisperer, why do you keep your companion a secret?"

"I'm not a Whisperer," said Tuanne, narrowing her eyes. "I am a hunter of the Red Sands tribe."

It was true she looked every bit the hunter, from her tough leather boots to her bow and quiver.

"Just because you weren't sent to train, it doesn't mean you aren't a Whisperer. You were chosen at birth just like me. A white feather was dropped at your door, wasn't it?"

Tuanne ignored Nara, turning her head to her companion. "Nimbus, calm down. It's time to go."

Nara watched them for a moment. She was used to being ignored by her parents and sister, but this was different – Tuanne was like her. They could help each other.

"Did the raven come?" asked Nara. Tuanne became very still. She didn't answer. "Were you summoned to Meridar for the Whisperer council?" Nara continued.

Tuanne looked up at Nara. Her scowl was softened by doubt. "Yes, the raven came," she replied. "It delivered its message, and then it left and life went on as normal. I'm not a Whisperer and I can't leave my people."

At that she turned her back on Nara and muttered something to Nimbus that Nara couldn't catch.

Nimbus crouched on Tuanne's shoulder for a moment before leaping down and darting away into the bush.

Nara watched the thorns shake as the monkey vanished.

"You can't whisper?" she asked Tuanne. "You can't speak your thoughts to each other?"

"I understand Nimbus perfectly well," said Tuanne, starting back towards the trail.

"But without words, how do you speak? How do you even know her name?"

Tuanne turned, glaring at Nara. "She showed me her name on our first meeting – an image of clouds rolling above the plains, the cloud that brings rain. It's called the nimbus cloud, the bringer of great gifts."

She tramped back on to the trail.

"I can teach you to whisper properly, if you want?" said Nara, following her. "You have the skill already inside you, you can—"

"Please," hissed Tuanne. "Don't speak about this. I'll be punished. They'll drive Nimbus away."

"Your mother?" asked Nara.

Tuanne glared at her, but the edges of her eyes glistened. She nodded.

Nara touched the girl's shoulder and walked on beside her. "I won't reveal your secret," she said. "I promise."

To speak, share and play with her companion was the greatest joy of Nara's life – for a Whisperer to be denied that seemed terrible to her. She quickened her pace to match Tuanne's so that they caught up with the rest of the group.

The ground dipped into a shallow valley and beyond that reared a great, shadowed cliff face. It was as if the earth had been torn apart and dragged up into the sky by an angry god.

The Demons' Door, said Flame.

Yes, said Nara. *And the Narlaw's hunting ground.*

At the head of the group Kalte stopped, turning for a moment and regarding Nara with a scornful look in her eyes.

"Whisperer!" she called. "Are you ready to enter the Rift?"

CHAPTER 5

The quickening rite had been passed down through generations of Whisperers in the savannah. It was a way of annointing weapons with the power of the earth and it was a skill that Nara had learned from Lucille. Once an arrowhead or a sword had been quickened it would become stronger and fly straighter. A quickened arrow could only be used by a Whisperer, but it was also one of the few things that could truly harm a demon.

Nara crouched a short distance from the rest of the group, beside a small fire that she had built. Her pack lay open on the rocky ground and Flame sat by her side, alert and on guard. The vast outer cliff face of the Rift rose at Nara's back, casting an oppressive shade over everything. The closeness of the Rift carried something else with it, too – an unpleasant thickening of the air that only a Whisperer could feel.

The fire crackled and Nara closed her eyes to begin the ritual. She lowered her first arrowhead into the flames and the words spilled from her mouth. She felt the arrow grow heavy in her hand and she knew that it was ready.

She placed this arrow carefully to one side and began on the next, glad to have Flame watching over her.

As she raised her final arrow from the fire Nara sensed a new tension through her bond with Flame. Someone was approaching from the group.

Nara placed the last arrow with the rest and looked up to see Tuanne standing shyly, a few paces from the fire.

"Does the magic work for all arrows?" Tuanne asked.

"It's not magic," said Nara. "It's Whisperer craft. The quickening doesn't last forever, and only a Whisperer can carry quickened steel."

Tuanne nodded, turning to the rest of the group and shaking her head.

"Wait," said Nara. "Bring *your* arrows."

Tuanne peered at her through suspicious eyes. She looked back to her mother for guidance, but her mother was too far away to have heard them.

"You want to banish the Narlaw?" said Nara.

"Of course I do."

"Well, these arrows can stop a demon in its tracks," said Nara. "No other weapon can do this. We stand a better chance with two of us carrying them."

Tuanne looked down at her feet for a moment. Then she slipped the quiver of arrows from her back and came to kneel beside the fire.

"Now close your eyes," said Nara. "We'll quicken them together."

Nara sent the ancient words into Tuanne's mind through the Whisperer bond and spoke them aloud at the same time. She could sense the girl's fear, but still Tuanne was receptive, mirroring Nara's speech as best she could. When all of Tuanne's arrows were ready, Tuanne returned to her mother and the rest of the hunters. Nara watched her go as she gathered her own arrows together and began smothering the fire with dirt.

The girl is too afraid of her mother, said Flame. *She's not ready for this – to fight as a Whisperer.*

Perhaps, said Nara. *But you can see how curious she is. She might even come north with us if we ask.*

You want to challenge Kalte for her own daughter? Flame snorted and began licking her paw.

Nara folded her pack and swung her quiver and bow on to her shoulder. *Maybe the tribe will understand,* she said, *once they've seen the Narlaw up close. Anyway, we'll need all the Whisperers we can get.*

As they rejoined the waiting hunters, Nara noticed how close Kalte was keeping her daughter. She fell in step with the group.

Ahead, a dark path awaited them.

The cliff face was cracked all over with fissures, some narrow and high up, sprouting with plant life, others at ground level like arched tunnels into the rock. It was into one of these tunnels that the lion tracks led them.

The four nomad hunters instantly spread out into a wary defensive formation. Kalte took the lead with Tuanne close behind. The girl looked worried and she peered behind her regularly. It would be hard for her companion, Nimbus, to follow her in here.

Two tall spearmen named Roho and Toum took the right and left flanks, and Nara and Flame brought up the rear. Nara drew her bow and nocked an arrow as she entered the cool, echoing dark.

The tunnel was several paces wide and, although it was utterly dark to begin with, there were pillars of sunlight ahead. Nara glanced up as they reached the first of them. The fissure they were passing through reached all the way to the summit of the Rift. Everywhere, cracks and tunnels branched off – it was a labyrinth. A place that could turn you around in an instant and trap you inside forever.

Nara reached out to Flame. *Tell me if you smell anything,* she said.

Many animals have passed this way, said Flame. *There's a foul odour, too. Not human or animal.*

Yes, I can feel it, too, said Nara.

Already the unnatural presence of the Narlaw was everywhere, just as her mentor had described it. It had settled like a stain on the rocks around them. Nara felt it like a physical sickness and she steeled herself against it. As they continued on their hunt, the demon taint would only grow worse.

Their footsteps echoed through the winding rock path, in and out of shafts of light, through tall caverns and sections of tunnel so low that Nara was only just able to stand upright. They moved swiftly, and Nara observed that the nomads seemed to know their way, moving confidently through the passageways.

They were deep inside the sprawling Rift when Kalte stopped abruptly and raised a clenched hand. Toum and Roho stopped in their tracks and Nara did the same. The tunnel was high-ceilinged, but covered over with vegetation at the top so that the light was dim and suffused with green. At the head of the group Kalte had unsheathed her sword. She crept forwards silently in a half crouch, which reminded Nara of Flame on the hunt.

Jackals, said Flame. *Lots of them.*

Nara raised her bow. It must be the same dog pack they had seen last night. She shuddered, remembering their hungry, desperate look.

Nara closed her eyes and reached out with her senses. She could feel the dogs creeping forward, but scattering pebbles and grit with their clawed paws. They were near, in an opening high on the left wall of the main tunnel. But the jackals' thoughts seemed skewed – scared and aggressive at the same time. They must have seen the demons. The whole pack was crazed and ready to attack anything.

Snarls of blind rage came echoing through from the side tunnel.

Nara opened her eyes. "Jackals are coming!" she called out. "Up high on the left!"

"Move!" cried Kalte, and together the group sprinted past the tunnel.

Toum dropped back behind Nara and Flame,

watching over his shoulder as the first of the wild dogs emerged. They leaped and tumbled down on to the trail floor. Nara turned and caught the eye of one snarling jackal. The creature's fear was obvious – this was the Narlaw's doing.

"Run!" bellowed Toum.

Nara didn't argue with him, charging ahead with Flame's paws thumping the rock beside her. They swept past Roho, who had fallen back to help Toum with the rear guard.

The manic sounds of combat bounced around the tunnel as Nara tried to catch up with Tuanne and Kalte. One of the spearmen cried out. Nara glanced behind, but a bend in the path had obscured everything.

"They need help!" she shouted to Kalte.

"Keep going," Kalte ordered. "We have larger prey to hunt."

"But—"

"I said keep going, Whisperer! We're here to banish demons not scrap with dogs."

The ferocity in Kalte's gaze was frightening, but

Nara slowed her pace anyway. She couldn't leave those two spearmen behind.

We have to help them, she whispered to Flame.

How? asked Flame.

Nara turned back the way they had come, her heart hammering in her chest. But before she could decide what to do, paws came thundering along the bend in the tunnel. A wiry, muscular jackal sped around the corner. Then another. And another.

Go! cried Flame.

Nara ran after Tuanne and Kalte, but the mother and daughter were nowhere to be seen. It took Nara a moment to realize that Flame wasn't running with her either. She stopped and turned back. Some of the jackals had got past Toum and Roho. They crowded the tunnel in a snarling pack, stopped in their tracks by Flame.

Flame commanded the tunnel, her tail flicking high and strong, her back arched ready to attack.

A jackal on its own couldn't hope to take on a leopard, but there were so many of them – ten at least. Nara watched in horror as the first of them leaped at Flame, but Flame dodged and swiped with one outstretched paw and the dog skidded away with a yelp. More came at her and Nara started back to help her companion.

No! whispered Flame. *Find Tuanne. Find the demons. Go!*

Flame threw herself at the oncoming jackals and the dreadful howl of battle filled the tunnel. The leopard reared on to her hind legs, swiping at everything that moved. Several of the dogs broke through, past Flame, and came charging at Nara with their jaws hanging wide.

All Nara could think was that if she ran, they would follow her and leave Flame alone.

"Come and get me!" she cried.

And she turned and fled along the tunnel.

CHAPTER 6

Through caverns and tunnels, Nara ran. The sounds of the stampeding, howling jackals were distorted by the jagged walls around her. She ran on, whispering Flame's name over and over, reaching out to her without success. She wondered where Tuanne and Kalte were … and Toum and Roho. She hoped they were all right.

Now that she was alone, Nara's thoughts turned back to the Narlaw – the lion-demons who had led them into the Rift. Nara felt the demons' taint everywhere. She wanted so badly for Flame to catch up with her, and to find Tuanne – and even Kalte, before the Narlaw appeared. But the further she ran, the more alone she felt.

She reached a fork in the tunnel. Her Whisperer

senses told her nothing useful about who or what lay down each path, so she trusted her instincts and took the brightest of the two. It wasn't long before the tunnel opened out into a vast, green-tinged cavern. There was even a slash of daylight at the faraway summit. Nara stopped at the cavern entrance, resting her lungs and peering about her, probing the shadows for life.

It was then she sensed the dogs. When they saw Nara – or smelled her, more likely – they dragged themselves up from the rocks and slowly drew together into a pack.

Nara reached for her bow. There were at least eight dogs ahead of her and her first thought was to turn and run. But where could she run to? There were more jackals behind her in the maze of tunnels. She reached out to Flame, but could only just feel her companion's distant presence.

Flame! she called. *Can you hear me?*

There was no response. Nara entered the cavern, thinking that perhaps she might be easier for Flame to find here in the open space. She kept her eyes fixed on the dogs and circled around the edge of the cavern towards a waist-high platform of rock. The jackals moved slowly, wary of her, but their intention to attack was perfectly clear. Nara climbed on to the platform, keeping the dogs in view, her bow drawn and a quickened arrowhead directed at the pack of scavengers.

"Flame!" she called out loud in desperation. Her voice bounced uselessly around the cavern and once it had faded, no reply came.

Nara's hand began to shake as the dogs slowly stalked her. She held the arrow as straight as she could, delaying the moment she would be forced to let it loose. Even though her life was in danger, she didn't want to do it. To harm an animal felt so wrong.

The lead jackal snarled and darted forwards in a mock charge, skidding to a halt near the base of the platform. A furious round of barking commenced, filling the cavern with noise. Nara steadied her arm. She had just six arrows in her quiver. Not enough, even if every shot struck home.

Then, suddenly, the dogs went silent. They backed away, still watching Nara, their eyes trained on the platform of rock.

Nara stared, too surprised to feel relief.

Only when she felt the sickening creep of the Narlaw did she realize what had happened.

She turned and saw their huge dark shapes descending from an opening above her. They stepped carefully down the crags and boulders. Their eyes glowed grey and the air in the cavern thickened with their evil.

Lions. Two females and a male, muscular and well fed.

Nara could not move.

Behind her the jackals fled, whimpering, from the cavern. Nara scrambled backwards, down from the rock platform and into the centre of the floor. She tried to breathe, telling herself that this was why she had joined with the nomads – to confront and banish the Narlaw. But she hadn't for a moment thought she would be doing it alone. She slowly backed away from the demons. It took every scrap of strength she had to resist the urge to run.

The Narlaw lions moved slowly and deliberately, spreading out across the cavern to encircle Nara. She trained her arrow on the lead female. This close, the lions' heads seemed impossibly large, their movements so heavy and strong.

The quickened arrows could only sap the Narlaw's power, not destroy or banish them. Nara delved into her memory for all that she knew of the art of banishment.

First she reached out carefully with her senses, but the touch of the Narlaw made her instantly recoil. The evil was so intense that her stomach lurched and she had to swallow hard. The lead female opened her mouth. Her teeth – *its* teeth – were long and yellowed. Its roar seemed to shake the cavern walls.

Nara squinted down the arrow shaft and let loose.

The arrow flew with a hiss, flashing through the air above the demon's lowered head and clattering on to the rocks beyond. Nara grabbed at her quiver in a panic. She was halfway to drawing her second arrow when the lioness pounced.

It sped forwards, huge paws thumping on the dirt.

Nara darted to her left and nocked the arrow as she ran. She spun.

The lion loomed at her with its demon eyes glaring and Nara loosed the arrow. Another miss.

She stumbled and rolled and scrambled up. The lion skidded to come after her. Nara glanced up at the other two. They were closing in, ready to trap her.

What would they do? She had heard about the ghost-sleep. But these were lion-demons – would they use their claws and teeth instead?

Nara launched herself up a small spur of rock, dragging her feet behind her as the air whooshed with a powerful paw swipe. She heard claws on rock, gravel falling. She climbed again, turned and fumbled for another arrow. The demon was already dragging its heavy torso up to meet her.

She looked around. "Flame!" she cried. "Someone!"

Desperation made her legs go weak. Behind her was nothing but sheer rock. There was nowhere else to go.

The lion rose, jumping up at the narrow spur. Nara backed up against the rock. She drew her third arrow slowly. The other two demons snarled and paced down below.

Nara pulled back the bow string. The demon was half on to the ledge, just three paces from her. This time she couldn't miss.

But the arrow that flew through the air and struck the lion was not hers.

The demon growled in rage, twisting in its climb. Nara stared across the cavern, seeing nothing. The arrow shaft stuck from the lion's shoulder. Its demon eyes dimmed.

Another arrow whistled and the demon fell.

Only then did Nara cast her senses out.

There, high up on the far side of the cavern, was Tuanne, scared but bitterly determined, the monkey, Nimbus, scampering to and fro at her side.

"We're coming!" Tuanne called.

She loosed another arrow. This time it struck the male lion-demon, causing it to roar with fury. It charged across the cavern and began climbing the rocks towards Tuanne.

"Look out!" cried Nara.

She still had her third arrow nocked and she spread her feet, carefully taking aim as the lion scrambled on the rocks. Her arm was steady now. A new hope and energy coursed through her.

The quickened arrow sailed across the cavern, dipping ever so slightly. The demon stumbled, struck in the side. Nara felt a guilty thrill of satisfaction as the creature slid from the rock face, back on to the cavern floor.

Tuanne looked tiny up there on the ledge, but her archer's stance was fearsome and so was her aim.

Below, however, the demons had regrouped. The two who had been hit were slow, but still moving.

Nara reached out, seeking to grasp the demon presences. She closed her eyes this time and felt for the earth's all-consuming power. All her life she had practised to perfect the earth trance. It was a

Whisperer's way of joining with the world and allowing it to act through her. She must become a channel so that it could reach up and expel the demons.

The trance came to her quickly – her technique was good. But nothing could have prepared her for the terrible sickness these three enraged demons would bring. Nara flinched, barely holding on to the contents of her stomach.

The demons split up and took to the boulders at the cavern edge to confuse her even more. Nara struggled to keep one or two in her sights, but she couldn't even pin them down.

Then she remembered. She was not the only Whisperer in the cavern.

Tuanne, she whispered. *Hear me.*

The girl's presence fluttered in surprise and beside Tuanne, Nara felt Nimbus, darting and anxious. Tuanne hadn't been trained. She didn't know how to whisper, but she had the gift – it was in her.

Reach out to me, said Nara.

She felt Tuanne grow ever so slightly closer. Nara bridged the gap, forgetting the Narlaw for a moment. Her contact with Tuanne was like a warm embrace, just as she felt when Flame was close.

Nara? Tuanne's voice was faint, untested.

I'm here, said Nara. *Follow my lead.*

As Nara sought the Narlaw once again she felt a familiar presence burn closer and closer. Flame sped into the cavern from the main tunnel entrance – graceful, quick and overflowing with relief. Next came Kalte, her presence prickly and warlike, then Toum, focused like an eagle in hunt and finally Roho, a rock of determination and strength.

You're safe, said Flame.

Thanks to you, said Nara.

Warmth flowed between them.

So, are you going to banish these brutes? said Flame. *Or do I have to chase them to the Darklands myself?*

Nara smiled. *Tuanne,* she said. *Now.*

Kalte and her men ran fearlessly for the lion-demons, as did Flame, drawing them out of their hiding places. The demons took the bait and, as they lunged into the open, Nara held tight to her bond with Tuanne, casting their powers towards the Narlaw.

The earth surged through her. It felt as if the cavern was filled with liquid heat. She felt every crack in the rock, every frond of moss and every dust mote in the air. The Narlaw became like insects in the face of the earth's protective might.

In a heartbeat it was done.

The cries of the nomad warriors rang out in surprise as the lions suddenly vanished. The echoes of battle died.

Thank you, Tuanne, Nara said, as she drew back.

She found the girl staring at her from across the vast cavern, wearing a look of absolute, delighted awe.

CHAPTER 7

Dawn sat awkwardly on the velvet-upholstered chair. Around her, on every available surface, candles flickered. Their shadow and light played across Princess Ona's fine features.

"Nothing." The princess shook her head in disbelief. "The demon took nothing."

"Are you sure?" asked Dawn.

Ona fixed her with a serious look. "I know my own wardrobe," she said.

Her ruined dressing room had been sifted through and her clothes taken to the laundry room. The princess's jewellery had been locked into newly built chests. Ebony had stayed for the whole procedure, sniffing for clues, but could only say for certain that it was Ona's jewellery the Narlaw had been most interested in.

"I want to ask you about the first time the Narlaw came," said Dawn. "When one took the form of your friend, Yusuf."

Ona nodded, but her eyes grew wide, as if it were still painful to think of those events. Dawn was sorry for dredging up bad memories, but she had no choice. If the Narlaw had not yet found what they wanted then they would almost certainly be back. She had to know what the demons were looking for and what the consequences might be for Meridina.

"Did the Narlaw ever come here?" she asked. "Into these rooms?"

"Yes," said Ona.

"And did it ask you anything? Did it seem interested in anything in particular?"

"I don't know," said Ona. "I mean, I thought it was Yusuf, one of my friends. Looking back, perhaps, it was more quiet than Yusuf would have been, but when we spoke it was about all the usual things – clothes, food, nothing really. You know how it can be."

Dawn nodded, although she couldn't remember the last time she'd had a conversation like that.

"Did he – it – ask to see your jewellery collection? Anything valuable? Any particular pieces?"

"I don't remember," said Ona. "Perhaps. Perhaps I showed him around the chambers and pointed out a few things. But I do that for everyone I like."

Dawn could sense Ona's growing agitation. The Narlaw had made a fool of her and it had trapped a good friend of hers in the ghost-sleep.

"Don't worry," said Dawn. "We have a lot to investigate already. You've been very helpful." She clasped Ona's hand and the princess smiled back.

"Thank you," said Ona. "For looking out for me. And for Yusuf. I wish I could do more."

Dawn smiled and rose from her chair. "Goodnight."

Outside she found Magda and two other Guards of the Sun.

"The Narlaw may return to find what it couldn't last night," she said in a hushed voice. "I'll be nearby this time. If it comes close, I'll feel it."

"Call for me if you do," said Magda. "I'd like to show this demon how the Guards of the Sun deal with intruders."

"I will," said Dawn.

She passed along the corridor until she was out of view and slipped into a small storage room.

Ebony was waiting at the window, silhouetted against the blue evening sky. *What news?* she asked.

The Narlaw didn't get what they wanted, said Dawn.

And the guards? Ebony probed.

Magda has interviewed the entire night watch and they have nothing to report. I have her notes – it seems no one saw or heard anything.

Strange, said Ebony. *Even for Narlaw.*

Yes, said Dawn. *So we must wait.*

Ebony hopped from the window ledge on to a high wooden shelf, displacing a small cloud of dust. *Indeed*, she said. *And what a perfect place to spend the night.*

The fine evening soon gave way to another noisy, rain-soaked night. Sharp droplets of water flew in through the high window, causing Dawn to drag her chair ever further into the dusty corner of the storage room. To fight the urge to sleep she whispered with Ebony, discussing the palace defences and the plans for the Whisperer council. When they both grew tired of that they began sharing stories from their homes, Dawn's from the dry, craggy hills of the Southlands, and Ebony's from high among the treetops of the western forests.

Neither of them noticed the eventual lull in conversation or their slow drifting towards sleep. So when Dawn felt a slick, tainted presence at the edge of her senses, she jerked upright in her chair and almost knocked Ebony from her shoulder.

It's here, Dawn whispered.

She stood.

Where? asked Ebony.

North. Twenty paces perhaps. I can't be sure.

She carefully opened the door to reveal the flickering torchlight of the corridor.

This way, she whispered, remembering her promise to Magda.

They hurried to Ona's chambers and found Magda standing at her post beside two other helmeted Guards of the Sun. Magda's eyes met hers and she knew instantly what was happening.

Dawn pointed towards the Narlaw presence – along a corridor at right angles to the one down which she had come. She held ten fingers up for the approximate distance, feeling it drawing nearer.

Magda silently gestured for the other guards to remain at the doors. She drew a short sword from the scabbard at her belt and nodded to Dawn, but as they crept forward, Dawn felt it stop. The demon had sensed her.

At that moment, footsteps rang out as the Narlaw fled. Dawn and Magda sprinted along the corridor, Ebony flapping awkwardly in the confined space.

Magda raced ahead, sword glinting in the torchlight.

"Intruder!" she bellowed.

Her cry was answered and repeated from a nearby guard station. Voices echoed through the halls as the alarm was raised.

Dawn pushed hard to keep up with Magda and when she swung round a sharp corner she found Magda had stopped at a junction. A set of steps ran up into darkness and a narrow corridor split away towards a separate wing of the palace.

"Which way?" asked Magda.

Dawn reached out. There was too much stone in the way. "I can't be sure," she said. "We'll have to split up. You and Ebony take the stairs and I'll go this way."

Magda nodded and immediately charged up the stairs, taking them two at a time.

Promise you'll call for me if you find it, she whispered to Ebony. *Don't let Magda tackle the demon alone.*

Only if you promise the same, said Ebony.

Dawn nodded and Ebony flapped after Magda as if she were her shadow.

Dawn started out along the corridor and, at first, it felt as if she was moving away from the Narlaw, but as she galloped down a short set of stairs and the corridor split once again she felt the demon there, just a few paces away.

Footsteps rang out to her left and Dawn set off. The low ceiling echoed with the thump of her boots, and those of the demon up ahead. Dawn stayed focused on the demon's presence, charging past low stone doors and the occasional wall-mounted torch. Every turn she took the Narlaw remained just out of sight. There was no one else around.

The corridor opened suddenly into a long, low-ceilinged room that Dawn didn't recognize. Huge wooden vats stood to either side and one solitary torch burned on the wall, halfway down the chamber. It was some kind of laundry room.

Dawn was several long strides into the chamber before she realized that she could no longer hear the demon's footsteps. She stopped dead. Her focus had strayed and the Narlaw could be anywhere.

She reached out again, cautiously. Just as she located the demon's presence, hiding behind a laundry vat, it charged out at her from the shadows.

Dawn leaped back, but not quickly enough. The demon crashed into her and she fell to the ground, twisting her ankle. Footsteps pounded away and Dawn peered into the semi-dark as she lay sprawled on the flagstones.

A dark cloak flapped.

Someone tall, a man perhaps.

And in the last instant before the demon slipped away Dawn caught a flash of red and gold beneath a cloak.

The uniform was unmistakable: a Guard of the Sun.

CHAPTER 8

The sound of drums filled the nomad camp – a joyful, tumbling rhythm that made it seem as if the flames of the great communal fire were not flickering but dancing. Nara sat cross-legged at the head of the long fire. Beside her, in a line, were Tuanne, Kalte, Toum and Roho. Flame lay sprawled behind her, gnawing on a bone, pausing only to stretch or yawn. Nara was exhausted, but the food and the music kept her awake and her spirits high.

This was a celebration. The Narlaw lions had been banished and soon the Red Sands tribe would gather the precious herds of cattle that had been scattered by the demons. The tribe would survive for another season.

The drums looped and thundered and Nara

found herself swaying along, watching in admiration as the dancers spun and dipped and whirled their arms in perfect unison.

Daan approached Nara and crouched before her, bowing slightly. "Remember," he said, "your request must be heard before the celebration fire turns to ember."

Nara nodded and thanked Daan again for the feast before he continued along the line of honoured warriors. It was customary for the Red Sands to grant one request to any outsider who had assisted the tribe, as Nara had done. Nara already knew what she would ask, and that it would not be received well. She must tread carefully.

She peered along to where Tuanne sat beside her mother. Nara tried to catch her eye, but failed.

Tuanne, she whispered. *Do you hear me?*

The girl's head jerked in Nara's direction and their eyes met. At first there was only fear in Tuanne's expression. She glanced at Kalte – worried, no doubt, that her mother would catch her in secret conversation with the outsider.

Look away, said Nara. *No one will know.*

Tuanne turned back to face the fire and Nara did the same. The great flames swayed and crackled. Sparks shimmered into the night sky and vanished.

I have a question, said Nara. *It is your choice, and you must do only what is right for you – but I want to know if you will come with me to the north.*

Tuanne didn't reply, but Nara sensed a nervous kind of interest in her.

When we banished the demons, said Nara, *I felt your strength. The kingdom needs Whisperers like you. I could teach you things as we travel. You could bring Nimbus, and learn to speak with her like I do with Flame.*

Nara felt a surge of excitement and longing from Tuanne. It was clear that she wanted to have her companion by her side more than anything, but to leave her tribe would be a huge upheaval, not just for Tuanne, but for Kalte and the rest of her family and friends, too.

Don't answer me now, said Nara. *I have until the celebration fire burns down to make my request to Daan. If you don't want to come then I'll ask for something else. Please, don't feel pressured.*

Nara glanced across and saw a troubled look on Tuanne's face. Then she caught the eye of Daan, who was crouching nearby. He was in conversation with another man, but all of his attention seemed to be focused on Nara. He watched her closely, as if he had guessed what her request would be. After a moment, he nodded at Nara, then he turned away, back to the conversation with his friend.

Nara leaned back, resting a hand on Flame's soft belly as she watched the fire. It was beginning to shrink in height, the logs of thorn wood falling in on themselves.

We should leave at dawn, Nara said.

Flame looked up from her meal. *And will we be leaving alone?* she asked.

We'll see, said Nara. *Let's enjoy the food and the dancing for now. It may be a long time before we see this kind of hospitality again.*

Flame licked around her muzzle with quick, rasping strokes of her tongue. She stretched her long limbs.

100

The food I can enjoy, she said. *But you know I'd rather sleep than dance. Will you wake me when it's morning?*

Nara smiled and scratched her friend behind the ears. *I suppose you've earned some rest this time.*

Flame curled up, laying her head on Nara's lap. Nara felt happy just to sit and observe as the people of the Red Sands celebrated. It was a huge victory for them – an enemy defeated, another season alive on the plains. But Nara couldn't help thinking of war. The message from the palace had been grave. A return to the dark times was threatening and war, if it came, wouldn't spare any corner of this beautiful, wild kingdom.

It was quiet when Nara woke. There were fewer people around the fire, which was now reduced to a few weak tendrils of orange amid the white ash and ember. Flame stirred at her side, shifting away from Nara and quickly finding a new position in which to fall back to sleep.

Nara slowly rose to her feet. She had not remembered falling asleep. A part of her felt embarrassed at having left herself so vulnerable to this group of strangers. But the Red Sands tribe were her friends now. Even Kalte's rudeness had disappeared since they had fought together in the Rift. She had clasped Nara's hand during the festivities and muttered a brief congratulation on performing the banishment.

Nara looked around. She had to find Tuanne and see if she had made up her mind whether to come with them or not. Then she would go to Daan and make her request. Although her stomach tightened nervously at the prospect, she knew asking Tuanne to join them had been the right thing to do. There were just a handful of Whisperers on the savannah, and even one new addition would help the kingdom.

Nara left the guttering fire in search of Tuanne, stepping carefully around others who had also fallen asleep in the grass. In the dark, her sense of direction failed her and she realized that she didn't know which tent belonged to Kalte and Tuanne anyway. But in the end, it didn't matter.

Daan approached her out of the shadows. "You've reached a decision?"

"Actually, I was looking for Tuanne," said Nara.

"Come," said Daan. "I'll take you to her."

Nara followed him through the moonlit trees. Daan was leading her towards his tent between the two tall acacia trees.

Inside, Kalte and Tuanne were waiting for them. Nara turned to Daan with a question on her tongue.

"Yes," said Daan. "Tuanne told us she wanted to journey north with you."

Nara caught Tuanne's eye, unable to suppress her grin. "And will the tribe allow her to leave?" she asked Daan.

"Yes," Daan said.

Nara turned back to Tuanne. "You're sure you want to come? If you don't then just say so. I'd understand."

Tuanne nodded, holding back on her smile. "I'm sure," she said.

"There are conditions," said Kalte. "Make careful note of them, Whisperer."

Daan nodded and stepped in. "Tuanne is in your charge," he said gravely. "You must see that she comes to no harm. Protect her with your life."

Nara nodded. "I will."

"And," continued Daan, "she must be returned to the Red Sands. This is her home and we are her people. You will make sure of that when the war is over."

Nara looked Tuanne in the eye, then Kalte. "You have my oath," she said.

Daan nodded and Kalte simply stared at the ground. Nara felt sorry for her – and guilty – despite her certainty that asking Tuanne to come with her was the right thing to do.

"Thank you," Nara said. "All of you. If we're to win against the Narlaw, we'll need girls like Tuanne."

Tuanne smiled then and Nara did, too.

"You're brave," said Kalte, "for a farm girl. And what you say about the war is true. Now leave us – Tuanne will find you at sunrise."

Nara bowed to each of them in turn and slipped out through the tent flap into the cool night. Excitement rushed through her as she rejoined Flame by the fire and lay beside her.

Flame stirred. *Well?* she asked sleepily.

We have sisters for the journey, said Nara.

Flame curled in tightly and Nara lay her head down, revelling in the warmth and softness. She let her friend's slow breathing lull her off to sleep.

CHAPTER 9

At daybreak Nara rose with the rest of the camp. The Red Sands tribe were moving on in search of their lost cattle and the camp was alive with activity. Tents came down to be rolled and packed and stowed in the saddlebags of the tribe's few tethered cows. Nara gathered her things together and nudged Flame awake. The sky shone a brilliant blue – the promise of a hot day.

It wasn't long before Tuanne found them. She wore loose, earth-coloured trousers and a long smock of a similar colour, along with her archer's gauntlet and leather shoulder pad. The pack she carried was compact, but well-stuffed. Her quiver of arrows had been refilled after the previous day's battle.

"I've said my goodbyes," she said. "We should leave now."

Her eyes were red from crying.

"Then we shall," said Nara, feeling the weight of the responsibility she had taken on.

Flame? she whispered.

Flame dragged herself up from the grass and stretched theatrically. *Always so early,* she complained.

Nara shook her head and Tuanne watched the two of them communicating in silence.

"Soon," Nara said, "you'll learn the pleasure of whispering. I only hope that your companion isn't as lazy as mine."

Tuanne smiled. "Nimbus is always moving. But I think monkeys need less rest than cats."

Nara shook her head. "Don't encourage her," she said, giving Flame a playful scowl.

The three of them passed among the people of the Red Sands. They drew many glances, some of the tribe nodding polite greetings to Tuanne, some coming over to hug her or shake her hand.

There were less friendly looks, too. Tuanne was a valuable tracker and one of the tribe's best archers. It was not hard to see why many would resent her leaving. But when the trio of travellers came across Roho, the warrior ran over and hugged both of them, giving his kindest farewell and his hopes for a safe journey.

They were soon out of the camp and following the dramatic cliff line of the Rift as it led them north-east. Their destination today was the river town of Heron's Bend, one of a cluster of small settlements along the banks of the Salesi. From there they would seek passage upriver to the edge of the Inland Sea. Nara calculated that a steady pace would bring them to the river by sunset. She strode along, pleased to be back on the move. In some ways their stay with the nomads felt like a dream. It was hard, even now, to believe that she had fought three Narlaw in the heart of the Rift and had performed her first banishment. But Tuanne, walking purposefully beside her, was living proof of what had happened.

Tuanne was very slim, but from the way she handled her bow, Nara knew she was strong. And although Tuanne was shorter than Nara, she managed to keep pace with her long strides.

Since they had cleared the camp, Tuanne had been casting her gaze around the bush.

"Do you feel her?" Nara asked. "Is she nearby?"

"I don't know," said Tuanne, slightly embarrassed. "Usually she finds me first."

"This is something else we can fix."

Nara cast her Whisperer senses into the undergrowth, between the trees and the boulders, up along the stony cliff face. There were many small creatures that might shy away from these passing humans and Nara felt them all, their presences faint or strong depending on their skill at hiding. There was movement away to the left, however – a halting, nervous scrabbling.

"There," she said.

Tuanne peered in the direction of Nara's outstretched arm.

A tuft of grass shivered.

Tuanne smiled. "Nimbus!" she called.

The monkey darted out of the bush, her tail curled above the red stripe of fur on her back. She crouched, surveying Nara and Flame.

"They're friends," said Tuanne. "Come."

Although Tuanne could not whisper, Nimbus understood her companion's feelings. She galloped on all fours, slapping the ground with her paws and jumping into Tuanne's open arms.

"You see," said Tuanne.

Nara sent a calm, friendly greeting to the monkey. Nimbus relaxed a little, but as they set off through the long shade of the cliff, the monkey dropped back to follow several paces behind the group, still eyeing Flame and Nara suspiciously.

A stretch of open grassland lay beyond the Rift. Fever trees rose above the grasses, spaced far apart like islands in a swaying yellow sea. They paused beneath a towering tree, enjoying food, rest and precious shelter from the searing midday sun. Flame loped off into the tall grass to hunt.

As they ate, Nara began to explain to Tuanne

some of the very first techniques she had been taught by her mentor – how to concentrate on her Whisperer sense, how to cast it out and feel for the presence of living things around her. She was surprised by how difficult it was to explain these things that came to her so instinctively now.

Although she had never been taught, Tuanne did already use her Whisperer senses to some degree. She had linked with Nara against the Narlaw in the Rift and she was skilled at feeling out her surroundings for potential danger or prey. By the time they were on their way again, Tuanne was casting out, calling the names of whatever she felt out there in the savannah.

"Ground squirrel!" she said. "Fifty paces east... Bee-eater birds in that thorn bush – three, no, four of them... A spring hare, look, you can see it, too!"

"You have a talent," said Nara.

And it was true. Tuanne seemed to know the species of whatever she sensed, even from far away. It had to be down to her childhood as a nomad, crossing the plains over and over, constantly at watch for predators, Nara thought. And there was her hunting experience, too. This was something Nara certainly didn't have. Her schooling told her that Whisperers should never kill, but Tuanne had been raised with different traditions, different ways of seeing the world. The nomads farmed no crops and hunting was a means of survival.

"A mongoose!" Tuanne called out. "It's digging into a termite mound."

Nara couldn't help but smile as a wave of sisterly affection swept over her.

By late afternoon they had left the Rift behind. The grasslands began to rise into a line of low hills, deep brown and golden in the dipping sun. It was from these hills that the four travellers got their first view of the river.

It curved across the flood plain, shimmering like a thick silver ribbon. The river towns clung to its edge, divided by a grid of irrigation channels that spread out across the broad, fertile plain. Only twice before had Nara travelled this far from home. For her, the Salesi river marked the edge of the known world.

Down on to the plain, they walked with renewed energy at the sight of the river – Nara and Flame side by side, and Tuanne a short way behind. Nimbus came and went from the group. Despite being born a companion, she had never properly lived with humans, and Nara was beginning to worry about getting this timid, distrustful creature on to a river boat for the next leg of their journey.

The flood plain was well-travelled, with paths and cart-roads that made the walking easy. There were many more insects here than any of the travellers were used to, however. Each of them walked with their hands, ears or tails flicking around their faces to ward the persistent, buzzing creatures away.

Several farmers greeted Nara as the group passed through. Her parents were well known here, and even though they rarely brought Nara with them on their trading trips, the presence of Flame made her easy to recognize. Flame paced warily at Nara's side.

Nimbus was even more nervous of the river people. She stayed close to Tuanne, often clambering on to her shoulder and wrapping her long tail around Tuanne's neck.

They reached the town of Heron's Bend as the sky was turning a deep, inky blue. There were enough houses for perhaps a hundred residents, all built from wood and lifted high above the earth on solid-looking stilts, ready for the seasonal rains.

Nara headed straight for the river banks and the wooden jetties that thrust out into the fast-flowing water. The place was busy at this hour, with a great many townsfolk returning from their days of trading or fishing. Flame and Nimbus drew many puzzled, wary looks. A pair of women paused from lifting a bulging net of fish out of their boat and nodded to Nara and Tuanne. A group of children running about on the river bank stopped to stare and several cowered at the sight of Flame, hiding behind the legs of their parents.

"Whisperer!" someone called from the end of one of the jetties. "Hey!"

Nara spotted a short man wearing a vivid green shirt waving at them from a small, sharp-prowed river boat. He was beaming at them as if they were long-lost friends, but Nara had never seen him before in her life.

What do you think? she asked Flame.

Flame narrowed her eyes. Her nostrils twitched. *He smells of mackerel,* she said.

I'm not asking whether you want to eat him, said Nara. *Do you think he's trustworthy? He seems to know who we are.*

Of course he does. How many other girls keep the company of leopards?

Nara nodded, studying the craft that sat gently bobbing at the end of the jetty. It was narrow and about ten paces long, with a short mast and a small covered section at the rear made from wooden stakes and sheeting. It seemed like a good a place to begin.

Tuanne drew up beside her. "I don't like this man," she said. "He smiles too much. On the plains we say that if a stranger comes smiling into your camp then he's surely hiding something."

"We'll see," said Nara. "Perhaps not every smiling man is a villain in disguise."

She led the way along the jetty, weaving around the workers and their stacked loads. The wooden slats sagged and creaked beneath her feet and the air was heavy with the smell of freshly caught fish.

"Greetings to you, Whisperer," said the man in green. He bowed, with his hands clasped together.

Nara couldn't tell whether this over-politeness was genuine, but when the man saw Nimbus he bowed to Tuanne.

"And another Whisperer," he said. "I am truly blessed today."

Tuanne gathered Nimbus into her arms and held her tightly, eyeing the man with unconcealed suspicion.

"Let me guess," the man said. "You're seeking passage north? To the Inland Sea or as far as I can take you?"

"How did you know that?" asked Nara. She looked for Flame, who was prowling around the edge of the jetty, sniffing at the boat.

"I've just returned from Kahsel, at the mouth of the river. My last passenger was a Whisperer. Her name was Lucille. Her companion was a wonderful black hawk."

Nara glanced down at Flame. Lucille, Nara's mentor, practised her craft in the scattered communities of the southern river plains.

"And you would go north again?" asked Nara, aware of Tuanne's warning gaze.

The man nodded, suddenly sombre. "Six years ago my baby son fell ill," he said. "A Whisperer cured his illness when no other healer could. My son would have died, but now he is a strong, healthy boy, and every day I thank the Whisperers for this blessing. I know why you must travel north – into great danger, and for the good of all of us here on the river. I am at your service." He dipped his head, eyes closed in reverence.

Nara glanced past him and saw Flame on his riverboat, scouring the planks and the bundles of gear with her nose. She looked up.

Yes, said Flame. *I think he is an honest man.*

Nara reached up and placed a hand on the man's shoulder. He raised his eyes.

"We'd be deeply grateful if you could help us reach the sea," she said.

The man smiled and held out his hand. "Marvellous!" he said. "I am Samuel. Very pleased to meet you."

"Nara," said Nara, shaking his hand. "And this is Tuanne. And Nimbus and Flame."

More courtesies were exchanged as they followed Samuel back along the jetty towards his home. They would depart at daybreak, he told them.

Although Nara was eager to continue the journey, she was exhausted from the miles they had travelled. And the dinner Samuel described in great detail as they walked really did sound delicious.

They approached a modest dwelling, raised on a complex scaffold of stilts, and Nara leaned in close to Tuanne as Samuel began climbing the steps ahead of them.

"Try not to worry," said Nara. "Trust doesn't come easily, but the more people you meet, the better your judgement will become. He's a good man. Flame can sense these things."

Tuanne nodded. "I'm so used to seeing all strangers as enemies," she said. "You have to, out on the plains. Life is different there."

"I know," said Nara. "Come, let's rest and eat."

They climbed the rickety wooden steps together, Tuanne holding Nimbus tight to her shoulder and Flame slinking silently behind them.

The welcome they received from Samuel's wife and son was every bit as warm as Samuel's had been. The boy could not take his eyes off the two companions, staring transfixed from Nimbus to Flame and back again. He was particularly interested in Nimbus, and Nara remembered how fascinated she had been the first time she had seen a monkey. Nimbus was so human-like in her expressions – a reminder that all animals, humans included, were not so different from one another.

Samuel cooked an extravagant meal as promised and they sat together, filling their bellies with delicious vegetables, fish and rice.

Night drew near and Nara and Tuanne gratefully took to their makeshift beds on the floor of the family's living space. The house creaked, swaying ever so slightly in the breeze.

As Nara lay down to sleep she listened to the smooth, persistent murmur of the great river. She thought of how she would soon be carried on its currents, away from her home and into the strange lands of the north.

CHAPTER 10

It was a bright morning, still dry, and Dawn sat on the balcony of her quarters with one leg up on a small stool. She could see the clouds gathering in the east, blown by the brisk, cold wind towards the capital for what was likely to be another rainy autumn day.

Her ankle spiked with pain as she shifted on her seat and reached for the fourth volume of Amina's war diaries. She had been stuck here since her run-in with the Narlaw, unable to join the search because of her twisted ankle and unable to sleep. Reading and worrying were all she had left. She wondered how many Whisperers would make it to Meridar. So far there were just five of them at the palace, including herself. She had barely enough Whisperers to search for the Narlaw spy, let alone fight a war. As she stared out from the balcony, she felt powerless and frustrated.

After Ebony and Magda had found her in the laundry chamber, lying bruised and barely able to walk, she had been carried upstairs and tended to by Moraine, a Whisperer from the north who was skilled at healing. Magda had agreed, with great disappointment, that the demon must have taken the form of a Guard of the Sun. How else could it have approached Ona's guarded chambers so boldly? Dawn had requested for each and every guard in the palace to be brought before her. Many had come and gone. But there were others still who were at their homes in the city or on duty elsewhere.

Dawn glanced up from her book as a shadow flitted across the outer wall of the tower, but it was not Ebony as she had hoped. She had sent the raven to the barracks of the Guards of the Sun to see if she could sense the Narlaw intruder there, although neither of them held out much hope. The demon would surely have fled into the depths of the palace. There were so many places to hide, so many places even Dawn's Whisperer sense could not reach.

The girl from the mountains, Alice, and the other two newly arrived Whisperers were scouring the palace grounds bit by bit. But still there was no news.

Dawn went back to her book. If she couldn't help in the search then she could at least try to figure out what the Narlaw were so desperately seeking in the princess's chambers.

She flipped to a passage near the end of the volume. It was a page she had read many times, in which Queen Amina described the final banishment of the Narlaw. That page was now marked with a slip of paper on which Dawn had scribbled the word *earthstone*. She sat back in her chair and re-read the lines of neat, handwritten script:

There were close to a hundred Whisperers in the circle and we were spread across several miles of hillside, but when we channelled together it was as if we were one being, a single part of the living world. I recall the sensation of warmth and of losing myself. My body was without weight and seemed to glow with the power that passed through me. Even the earthstone shone within its bindings, a brilliant blue-white like the sun reflected on the surface of a deep, pure lake.

The moment itself is hard to describe. Imagine a piercing cry that seems to fly from every blade of grass, every wisp of air, every tiny pebble in every river – the whole of the wild earth screaming in defiance of the darkness in its midst. This is my best attempt at conveying such a feeling with these poor and clumsy words of mine.

Afterward came silence. The demons were gone. Each one of us could feel it. A weight had been lifted from the world.

Dawn lowered the book and stared blindly into the morning sky. The passage never failed to move her. It was such a pivotal moment in the history of Meridina – in the history of the Whisperers. But on this reading there was more to think about.

The earthstone. Dawn had seen it mentioned before and had marked pages in Amina's war diaries. The stone was only ever mentioned in passing and for this reason Dawn had taken it for a favourite trinket or a royal heirloom of some sort. Now she was not so sure.

The interest the Narlaw had shown in Princess Ona seemed puzzling at first, but what if they were looking for something powerful, some vital artefact that Ona had inherited from Queen Amina?

First had come the Yusuf-demon, its form chosen perhaps because of Yusuf's closeness to the princess. And now a member of the Guards of the Sun, the soldiers whose duty it was to keep Ona safe and her chambers secure.

Dawn climbed slowly to her feet, grasping at the sturdy wooden crutch that had been brought to her from the infirmary. She needed to speak to Ona, to find out what she knew about the earthstone. Its descriptions were so vague in Amina's diaries, and it seemed that it was a different colour at each mention.

If only Ebony were here, Dawn could have sent a message right away, but she would have to make do with one of the guards who patrolled the corridor outside. Before Dawn could draft a note to the princess, there was a knock at her door.

Valderin strode in. "I have news," he said.

"You found the demon?" asked Dawn.

Valderin shook his head grimly. "The Narlaw have broken cover in the middle lowlands and an army is coming towards the capital. They've already surrounded the city of Altenheim. There's a Whisperer there, trapped by the fighting. Her hawk companion flew here to warn us."

Dawn stared back at the guard captain, unable to speak for a second. "We don't have an army yet," she said.

"No," said Valderin. "So far, there are only local militia outside the capital."

Dawn bowed her head. Two towns already gone. And how many townspeople sunk into the ghost-sleep? How many more Narlaw spilling across from the Darklands to take on human form?

"We must go to them," said Dawn. "How quickly can the palace guard be ready?"

"Preparations are already under way," said Valderin. "We will ride out today. Now, if you'll excuse me, there is much to be done."

Dawn thanked him as he left. Ona and the earthstone would have to wait. First she must assemble the Whisperers and join Valderin in preparation for war. She thought about riding into battle, how it would feel in the presence of so many demons – a whole army of them. She thought of Queen Amina's linked circle of Whisperers and how few there were at the palace now. No one had expected the Narlaw to advance so quickly across the kingdom. But it seemed they had learned from their defeat a hundred years ago and were trying to strike before the Whisperers could unite.

Dawn hobbled back to the balcony, looking to the skies for Ebony. She was so very unprepared. Perhaps the warden had been right … the kingdom needed a real leader, like Queen Amina, not some clueless girl from a southland village. Dawn closed her eyes and laid a hand on the leather-bound cover of the war diaries. She pressed down hard, as if some fraction of Amina's strength could be transferred to her through paper and ink alone.

CHAPTER 11

Nara rose early and went out on to the veranda of the stilt-house, stepping carefully around the sleeping forms of her companions. In the soft glow of dawn she caught sight of Samuel down on the jetty, preparing for the journey. Isolated clouds scudded across the sky, creating subtle shadows on the silvery surface of the river. Nara breathed the cool morning air and looked north to where the Salesi dwindled and vanished on the far horizon.

Tuanne, Flame and Nimbus did not stay asleep for long – Samuel's boisterous son made sure of that. He woke Nimbus by gently taking hold of her tail. The monkey screeched in surprise and leaped from where she had been sleeping – straight up into the rafters of the house. She darted to and fro above their heads, accompanied by the boy's good-natured laughter.

Tuanne scowled at the boy and tried to draw her companion back down.

Flame rose drowsily, watching all of this with irritation as she stretched her long limbs and flicked her tail.

Eventually, they were able to eat a quick breakfast together. Then they joined Samuel on the jetty.

Nara had ridden in a boat once before – a river crossing with her parents – so she knew what to expect. But Tuanne had never been afloat before and she clambered in, wide-eyed and stiff-limbed, clutching at Nara and then at the mast before quickly dropping on to one of the seating planks. Nimbus immediately scampered into the small, covered storage area at the back of the craft and hid between the waxed sacks and coils of rope. Flame simply sauntered on board and found the driest place she could in which to curl up and doze.

When all four of them were settled, Samuel clapped his hands together.

"We have fine weather today," he announced. "The river will carry us swiftly to Kahsel!"

He unwound the rope from its mooring and pushed them away from the jetty. The boat swayed, spinning slightly before being gathered by the downstream current. Its narrow prow straightened, spearing through the shining water. They were on their way.

Nara realized that she was further than she had ever been from home. She had barely had time to think about her family since leaving, but now, on the sudden quiet of the river, her thoughts became clear.

Would her parents miss her?

Nara had said goodbye to her father and she wished she had done the same for her mother and sister. But they had known she was leaving at dawn and they had not come to see her off.

She gripped the edge of the boat and watched the tall houses of Heron's Bend disappear from view. Samuel's family so obviously cared for each other. And they appreciated the Whisperers, too. Nara felt anger rise in her at the way her own family had refused to value her craft. She felt a new determination to prove herself, to show that she could help save the kingdom no matter what anyone thought.

She held that feeling tight as she moved to the front of the boat to sit beside Tuanne. They both watched Flame, who had taken to leaning against the prow, revelling in the breeze with her eyes closed and her ears flat against her head.

"She's enjoying herself, at least," said Tuanne with a half smile.

"Yes," said Nara. "Flame has a talent for finding the most comfortable spot in any situation."

"You know each other well," said Tuanne.

Nara nodded. She glanced back at the storage area. Samuel stood behind it, controlling the tiller, and Nara felt Nimbus's presence there, too, small and nervous, hidden from sight.

"Now you and Nimbus are together," said Nara, "you'll find it easier to whisper. You'll soon know each other like Flame and I do."

Tuanne squinted at the moving riverbank.

"I feel so far behind," she said. "I need to practise controlling my senses or I'll be useless as a Whisperer when we reach the north."

Nara nodded in sympathy. She knew from her life on the farm how it felt to be out of step with those around her. But she also felt a strong pulse of happiness – Tuanne had referred to herself as a Whisperer for the first time.

"You're already good at recognizing animals by their presence," said Nara. "Maybe this is a way to control your senses?"

It was a difficult exercise. They were travelling at some speed and the creatures around them were quick and skittish – the fish of the river, the birds and reptiles of the riverbanks. But Nara listened with pride as Tuanne gradually picked them out, focusing on those quick, blurry presences and interpreting their forms.

Tuanne kept working – casting out her senses, pushing further, pulling back and pin-pointing even the tiniest, most evasive creatures. The sun climbed across the sky and the two Whisperers only stopped their work to eat or to wave to people on passing boats.

Samuel had been right about the weather. What little wind there was came from the south, allowing him to unfurl the boat's small triangular sail and gain some extra speed. It also kept the travellers cool and helped rid them of the pestering insects that inhabited the river lands.

It was mid-afternoon when the Salesi began to widen and the first outskirts of Kahsel became visible through the heat haze. Small waves started to lap at the boat's sides, growing ever more forceful. Both girls held on to the bench beneath them and Flame drew back from the prow to sit, alert, at Nara's feet.

"It's choppy today!" Samuel called from the stern. He sounded excited rather than concerned. But he was used to the water and Nara imagined that he could swim, too.

Nara leaned close to Tuanne. "Can you swim?" she asked.

Tuanne shook her head.

"Me neither," said Nara.

They both gripped the wooden bench a little tighter.

They plotted a course along the eastern bank, careful to avoid the larger vessels that were moored there. Kahsel was the largest settlement Nara had ever seen. Its wood and earth-brick buildings crowded the long curve of the eastern shore, right round to the beginnings of the Inland Sea. Tiny ferryboats went to and fro across the river mouth like lines of ants, men and women labouring at their oars, decks piled high with cargo or crammed with foot passengers and livestock.

Samuel steered them expertly into a lively section of the docks. Boats bobbed and bumped together. Traders and passengers clambered about in an incredible rush. Everyone seemed to be shouting and Nara could sense Tuanne's unease.

"Don't worry," Nara said, grasping her hand, although she couldn't help but feel anxious herself. She had never been surrounded by so many people, such noise and activity.

Samuel climbed past them to the front of the boat, securing it to the dock with a coil of rope.

"Stay here," he said. "I'll be back soon. Don't leave the boat."

He pushed away through the crowds.

Tuanne turned to Nara. "Where's he going?" she asked.

"I don't know."

Nara looked down and saw that Flame was gone. She glanced around, suddenly panicked. But Flame had simply moved to the rear of the boat. She was hunkered down in the shade of the storage space with Nimbus, both of them peering out at the masses of bustling, shouting people. If the docks were an unnerving place for Nara, then she knew they would be twice as bad for the animals.

Luckily, they didn't have long to wait – Samuel soon returned.

"Come," he said. "I've secured you passage on a freighter. It leaves in one hour."

He held his hand out and Nara reluctantly rose to her feet. She straightened as the boat wobbled beneath her. Now was the time to be strong. She remembered her oath to the Red Sands tribe.

"Let's go," she said to Tuanne.

As Tuanne rose and took her hand Nara glanced back at Flame.

Are you ready? she asked.

If I must, said Flame.

Flame turned and poked her nose into Nimbus's hiding place. Nara couldn't tell what passed between the two, but when Flame padded down the length of the boat, she had Nimbus by her side.

Tuanne reached down and took her companion in her arms, stroking the tufted white-and-red fur of the monkey's back. She nodded, and the four of them climbed from the boat and followed Samuel into the throng.

Although Flame drew plenty of astonished looks, the people of the docks were far too busy to stop and stare. Nara strode and side-stepped and jostled her way through behind Tuanne. Samuel looked back often to make sure they were still with him and when they reached the freighter he took Nara's hand and bowed solemnly.

"Thank you for your kindness," said Nara. "We are indebted to you."

"There's no need for thanks," Samuel replied. "The only debt is my own."

He introduced them to the captain of the freight ship – a quiet, stocky man who was too busy with the loading of cargo to do more than glance and nod in their direction.

They left Samuel on the dock and climbed the narrow gangplank on to the broad deck of the ship. Where Samuel's vessel had been sleek and quiet, this one was vast, laden with casks and crates. It was loud, too. Men and women stomped across the deck and shouted to each other as they carried great coils of rope or metal pulleys as large as a person's head. The deck hung several paces above the level of the dock and its three great masts rose much higher still. Ropes dangled everywhere, knotted around sails and more were coiled in huge piles all about the deck. The ship was called the *Wandering Star*.

"This way," muttered the captain, appearing

beside them and taking Nara by surprise.

He led them into one of several low, cramped cabins built up at the rear of the ship. Nara glanced back at the dock and waved goodbye to Samuel before he slipped out of view. She wished he was coming with them.

The *Wandering Star* left Kahsel docks in the first cool hour of the early evening. There was a great clamouring and shouting aboard, and Nara stood in the cabin doorway to watch the crew run, lift and drag the sails into position. Meanwhile, the crews of two large rowing boats heaved the ship out of the busy harbour. The long towing ropes creaked and Nara watched the grimacing rowers, amazed at their strength. As the ship entered open water and the support boats bobbed away to the sides, Nara looked out to sea. There, ahead of her, was nothing but water – no land on the horizon, just green and white waves fading to a hard, deep grey like hammered lead.

I hope the Middle Country is ready for us, said Flame, appearing at Nara's side.

Nara placed a hand on her friend's head and stroked her distractedly. *I never imagined it could be so far,* she said.

No, said Flame. *These are strange times to be a Whisperer. We must be ready for anything.*

Night fell and the waves of the Inland Sea rose and crashed against the *Wandering Star* with relentless fury. The ship's crew yelled and grunted at their posts, struggling to stay on course and to keep the sails from tearing in the unpredictable winds. The captain bellowed as he walked among them.

In the cabin it was impossible to sleep. No one was spared from the seasickness, and Tuanne and Nara took turns dashing out of the flimsy cabin door to empty their stomachs over the rail. Halfway through the night Nara returned from outside to find Tuanne in a terrible panic.

"Nimbus!" she cried. "She's gone. Have you

seen her? Have you seen Nimbus?"

"Where would she go?" asked Nara.

Nimbus had hidden beneath the corner bunk of the cabin as soon as they had boarded, but she was no longer there. The cabin was tiny. There was nowhere else to hide.

"She must have gone outside," said Tuanne. "There's a storm! Maybe she's been washed over the side…"

Nara grabbed Tuanne by the hand. "We'll find her," she said. "We're Whisperers, remember?"

Tuanne met Nara's gaze, utterly distraught. But she nodded.

"Come," said Nara. "Reach out with me."

They left the cabin, lurching across the narrow gangway and grasping the railing as the ship tilted and sea spray blasted over them. Flame slinked out of the cabin behind them, adding her keen eyes, ears and senses to the search. All of the sails were down and few of the crew remained on deck. There was nothing to be done now but ride out the storm.

Nara darted to the base of the main mast and threaded her arm through a loop in a tight coil of rope, gesturing for Tuanne to do the same. Together they closed their eyes and cast out with their senses.

Nara felt little besides Flame and Tuanne at her side and the crew – tucked away in their quarters or stoically manning their posts. Beneath the sea there were shimmers of life, but the sickening movement of the deck kept her from focusing on anything for long.

She whispered to Tuanne. *What do you feel?*

Tuanne radiated urgency and fear. Moments passed before she replied.

Up, she said simply. This was only the second time Tuanne had tried to whisper to Nara. *The mast,* she said.

They looked up together and there, clinging to the rigging with all four feet and her tail, was Nimbus.

Whisper to her, said Nara.

"I can't," Tuanne shouted.

Words are nothing but vessels of meaning, said

Nara. *Speak that meaning to your companion. Ask her to come down.*

Nara clung to the mast and waited as the storm howled around them. She glanced down at Flame, who crouched beside her with her fur slicked flat by the wet. She seemed almost as worried about Nimbus as Tuanne.

When Nara looked back at Tuanne she had Nimbus wrapped around her shoulders.

"I'm not sure," Tuanne shouted, "but I think she said she was bored!"

"Bored?" Nara's laugh was instantly dragged away on the wind. "You have a strange one there," she shouted.

The monkey tilted her white-tufted head at her as if taking offence.

Tuanne unhooked her arm from the mast. "Shall we go?" she said.

Nara smiled, and she and Flame followed the other two along the lurching, spray-soaked deck.

At some point during the night the storm must have blown itself out, because Nara woke to a tranquil, gently swaying cabin and the surprising knowledge that she had managed to sleep. From outside she heard the crying of gulls. A crack of bright light shone beneath the cabin door.

Before Nara could even sit up on her bunk there was a thump at the door.

"Wake up, ladies! You made it!"

Nara stumbled on to her feet, rearranging her clothes. She threw open the door and stood dumbstruck. Ships of every kind filled the dark green sea – too many to count. Above them birds wheeled in a grey-blue sky and, beyond that, sprawling over steep hills, was a city the likes of which Nara had never seen. Everything was made of stone, even the huge walls of the docks, a heavy-looking grey that gave the impression of strength and defiance.

She glanced along the rail and found the captain leaning there, staring out at the city. A smile creased his sunburned face – the first she had seen since boarding the ship.

"Welcome to Endhaven," he said, without turning his head. "The Middle Country." Then he spat into the sea and strolled away in perfect rhythm with the rolling of the deck.

CHAPTER 12

Kahsel had been shocking enough in its clamour and chaos, but Nara's arrival in Endhaven felt like being cast into an entirely different world. Everything was different – not just the imposing grey stone of the buildings, but the people, too – their faces and their clothes, their ways of speaking. As Nara passed tentatively along the docks, leading her friends in single file, she felt both dread and excitement at being so very far from home.

They dodged through the bustle of traders, passengers and dockworkers. Packhorses clopped and stamped, waiting for cargo or dragging it away into the city in teams. The cobbles underfoot were slippery and damp, as if it had recently rained. Nara had heard about this – how it rained all year round in the north. How did people plan their crops with such weather?

She stopped to let a fast-moving wagon pass and looked back to check everyone was still there. Tuanne had a wild, defensive look in her eyes and was clutching Nimbus close to her chest.

Flame looked around suspiciously. *This place smells awful*, she said.

I know, said Nara. *Too many people.*

They crossed the docks and plunged into a narrow uphill street that ran directly north. It was impossible to walk at any speed with so many people around, and Nara peered into the dingy openings of shops and alleyways as she shuffled past them. Faces glanced or glared or stared back at her blankly.

"Need a ride, dear?" A man dressed in shabby clothes had appeared in front of her, walking backwards as he talked. "Somewhere to stay?" he asked.

"No," said Nara. "Thank you."

"Where you headed?"

"We're meeting someone," she lied.

He sidestepped out of her way without further comment.

As they left the *Wandering Star*, Nara had asked the captain where they might find transport towards Meridar. The Corn Exchange was where the northbound carriages waited, the captain had said, and nothing more. Now all they had to do was find it.

At the top of the hill, the street opened out into a small square. Lanes and alleys led off in all directions. Nara stopped, and she and Tuanne were barged and cursed at by those trying to pass through. Flame crouched, growling quietly, and the few passers-by who spotted her gave the group a wide berth.

Nara tried to stop someone to ask directions and, on the third attempt, an elderly woman carrying a vat of something that smelled revolting finally paused to help. The woman raised her arm wordlessly towards another narrow street before hobbling on her way.

When they finally made it to the large open

square that was the Corn Exchange, Nara led them to a quiet corner.

"We need to find a carriage that can take us to Meridar," she said. "I'll ask around. Perhaps I should do that on my own…"

I'll be glad to stay out of the crowds for a while, said Flame.

Nara looked at Tuanne, who nodded. She had barely spoken since disembarking.

"This place," Tuanne said. "It makes me nervous. The noise and the people – the way they stare at us."

"I know," said Nara. "But we'll be free of it soon. I'll find a carriage to take us to the capital."

"Couldn't we walk?" asked Tuanne.

"It's too far – we need to move fast. Who knows how far the Narlaw have pushed into Meridina by now."

Tuanne reluctantly agreed and Nara set off on the hunt for transport. She scanned the square and spotted ranks of carts and carriages on the far side. She took a deep breath and strode across. Very soon, she realized that they were in trouble. Between them, they had no money. The coach drivers asked her what she did have, nodding at her bow and arrows, sometimes even asking about the value of the animals. Nara carried on, but with a sinking feeling. No one cared that she was a Whisperer – or that the palace would no doubt pay for the journey on her arrival. It wasn't until she reached a final cluster of carriages that Nara met with someone who could help.

Her name was Bryony, a stout middle-aged woman with short sandy hair and an air of good-natured cycnicism. "Don't listen to them – they're only out for themselves," she said. "As far as this ignorant lot are concerned, the Narlaw don't even exist. Just because they haven't seen any demons yet, they think everything's just fine."

Nara liked her immediately. "Have you heard any news from the north?" she asked.

"Only that some Narlaw have crossed the mountains," said Bryony. "And the palace are calling in the regional militias for training. It looks like war's coming."

Nara nodded gravely and felt a sharp chill of fear.

Within the hour they were trundling through the outskirts of Endhaven, into a land of rolling green hills, hedges and woodlands.

I guess this is what all the rain is for, Nara murmured to Flame.

Flame lay beside her on the hard bench of the carriage. *Green is all very well*, she said. *But how is a cat like me supposed to hunt in it?*

Nara smiled. *You do stand out a bit.*

She looked across at Tuanne, jostled by the bumping of the cartwheels. Nimbus had crept beneath the bench, curled behind Tuanne's pack and her quiver of arrows. The little monkey was watching Flame, her black eyes shiny and alert and her white-and-red fur tufting out untidily.

The cart was uncovered and, although the sky felt low and heavy compared to the vast shimmering blue of the savannah, Nara began to feel herself relax again.

They stopped for lunch in a copse of trees on the edge of a quiet village – so quiet, in fact, that it seemed almost deserted. Bryony said it was because of the Narlaw. Word of the invasion in the north was spreading, and people had begun to move south, leaving their homes in fear of a coming war. Whatever the reason, finding food in the village proved difficult and their midday meal was sombre and unsatisfying.

Only Bryony seemed in high spirits, regaling the group with tales of the rude, ungenerous and strange passengers she had carried over the years. Nimbus's spirits looked to be improving, too. She scampered over and sat with Flame as the others ate, watching the big cat closely as she rested in the dappled shade.

They drove on and Nara suggested to Tuanne that practising her whispering might distract them as they travelled. Tuanne listened carefully as Nara explained how she had been taught by her mentor. Then Tuanne tried her best to send the meaning of her thoughts across her bond with Nimbus.

You have to listen, too, said Nara. *Nimbus wants to whisper to you just as much as you do to her.*

Search the bond for your companion's thoughts.

The sky darkened and a drizzle of rain set in. Bryony handed out a pair of old blankets, which Nara and Tuanne spread over themselves, letting Flame and Nimbus shelter between their feet. They passed more villages and one large town with even fewer people in its streets than any before. The only other travellers they saw on the road were heading south.

At one point they passed what seemed to be a whole village on the move. Five or six carts were fully laden with people, furniture, sacks of belongings and caged hens. The refugees nodded solemnly to them and Nara nodded back.

Up front, Bryony shook her head and muttered to no one in particular.

Shortly after that they came across the first signs of Narlaw.

The rain had stopped and they had just crossed a long, stone bridge over a river. Tuanne was deep in her Whisperer trance, and Nara was alternately watching Tuanne and the roll of the hills on the horizon.

Nara sensed the poisoned earth before she saw it. Her stomach tightened. Tuanne woke suddenly from her trance and Flame stirred beneath the bench. Bryony stopped the cart and together they stared at the desolation.

The hillside was in ruins. All grass, crops and hedgerows were gone, replaced by a cracked desert of mud, pooled with dirty rainwater. A copse of what used to be trees lay like bones halfway up the hill, white and lifeless. There was a farmhouse not far from the road. Its roof and windows were gone and its stone walls were blackened with fire damage.

How many demons came through here? Flame asked.

I don't know, said Nara.

She followed the broad swathe of devastation by eye. It led north-east, across the road and over the low hills on the other side of the valley.

It's not so bad over there, she said, pointing to the east. *Perhaps they stopped here to feed.*

Nara realized that Tuanne and Bryony were watching her, awaiting a decision.

"We should carry on," she said. "This will be the fate of the whole kingdom if the Whisperers don't unite."

Bryony lowered her head and nodded.

Tuanne reached down and took her bow in her hand.

"We can't fight this many," said Nara. "We'll need to be clever to find a way through to Meridar."

"And if the demons find us?" said Tuanne. She gripped her bow as if she meant to banish the Narlaw army with her arrows, one by one.

"If they find us," said Nara, "then we will have to fight."

For the remainder of the day the road led them north. They stopped only to water the horses, sharing out what few provisions Tuanne and Nara still carried in their packs and eating as they rode. They didn't cross the trail of the Narlaw again, although Nara was wary. She kept her senses trained on the hills and woods around them and she knew from Tuanne's posture that she was doing the same. Her training would have to wait.

Evening came and a cold rain set in. Nara drew her blanket close and was glad of Flame's warmth around her legs. As the daylight dwindled they entered a market town. The houses were made from the same grey stone as the other settlements they had passed and the roofs were either thatched, much like Nara's own in the savannah, or else constructed from overlapping slates. Nara watched the shadows between the houses and reached into the buildings with her senses. This town was also deserted. She felt for signs of Narlaw, but found none. Then a door banged loudly somewhere off to her right and Nara jumped to her feet. Flame scrambled out from beneath the bench, ready to attack, and Tuanne stood with an arrow trained towards the sound.

"Don't shoot! Don't shoot!" A man emerged from the darkness between two cottages. He held his hands up in a gesture of surrender and the sleeves of his battered old coat hung raggedly. His face was dirty and bearded and it was impossible to guess his age. "You're Southlanders," he said.

"What of it?" demanded Tuanne. Her bow string creaked as she tensed.

"I meant no disrespect," the man asked. "But you are Whisperers, no?" He stepped closer. There was a glimmer of hope in his tired, anxious eyes.

"We are Whisperers," said Nara. "Who are you?"

The man exhaled in relief and dipped his head. "Thank the stars," he muttered. He looked up. "I am Olmar, a scout from the city of Altenheim. I was sent for help, to find more of you. They said you would be coming."

"Where did you say you were from?" asked Nara. "Who said we were coming?"

"From Altenheim – it is three miles from here," said Bryony. "It's the main settlement in these parts."

"We're under siege," said Olmar. "The demons came three nights ago. They have us surrounded. One of your kind is with us – Lucille. She said there would be more of you coming, but I'd given up hope…"

Nara and Flame shared a look at the mention of Nara's mentor.

Olmar came forwards and laid his hands on the edge of the cart. His eyes burned with desperation. "Please," he said. "We weren't prepared for this. Our city is nearly overrun."

Nara reached a hand out and helped him on to the cart. "Come, sit," she said. "Bryony, is Altenheim on our way?"

"It can be," said Bryony.

Olmar clambered into the cart and perched on the end of the bench. He shook Nara and Tuanne's hands. Then he gave Flame and Nimbus a quick glance each. "I never thought I'd be sharing a cart with such fine creatures," he said.

That earned him a gracious nod from Tuanne.

"You say Lucille is with you?" Nara asked the man.

He nodded.

"Then we have to get to her," said Nara.

"And what about our palace summons?" Tuanne asked.

"We were summoned," explained Nara, "to help defeat the Narlaw. We will do our best to get there, but it seems the war has already found us."

A gust of cold rain blasted across the cart and Nara drew her blanket tight around her shoulders. She edged her way to the front of the cart and leaned close to Bryony. "I know it's asking a lot," she said. "But would you take us to Altenheim."

Bryony tilted her head as if weighing up Nara's request. She squinted into the rain. "I've seen just about everything else under the sun," she said. "So why not drop in on some demons, eh?" She smiled mischievously and nudged the horses into motion, and into the dark, wet onset of their first northern night.

CHAPTER 13

Altenheim was lit by fire. From a low ridge to the south the travellers watched flames flicker on both sides of the high city walls. The river shimmered, red and orange over black. The night sky rang with the sounds of battle.

"The river gate," Olmar said, pointing. "It's the only way in since the demons took the lands to the west. Everything outside the walls is lost."

Nara peered down the river valley. Altenheim occupied the western shore of a wide river. The one bridge that led into the city had collapsed.

"You have a boat?" she asked Olmar.

"Hidden on the east bank," he said. "We'll ford the river here and re-cross into the city. Keep your eyes open for demons."

"We can do better than that," said Nara, glancing at Tuanne. "You have Whisperers with you now."

Olmar nodded, a grim smile on his face.

He led them down the ridge under cover of a tangled stretch of woodland. Bryony had left them, taking her cart south to spread word of the Narlaw invasion. Nara's sandals sunk into the damp earth and leaf mulch. She ducked through thickets of thorny branches and Flame trod silently behind her.

The shallows of the river looked pure black in the moonless night. Olmar gestured them on and they crossed the ice-cold ford, pebbles rolling and clattering under their feet. On the other side Flame stopped to shake her fur dry.

I suppose I'm too big to carry? she asked Nara, glancing at Nimbus who was perched, perfectly dry, on Tuanne's shoulders.

Don't complain, said Nara. *Your fur will dry quicker than my clothes.*

A short way up river Olmar told them to wait on the edge of an overgrown meadow. He darted on ahead to make sure the boat was still there and Nara crouched beside Tuanne, peering into the long, dark grass beyond. She closed her eyes and cast out with her Whisperer sense. Night birds flickered between branches, some tiny creature rustled through the leaf litter close by. She sensed the unease and the watchfulness of each of her companions.

Nara, Tuanne whispered urgently.

Nara opened her eyes.

There, said Tuanne.

Tuanne's whispering was still a little clumsy, but her meaning was clear. Nara reached out and felt the form beneath the trees at the far end of the meadow. There was no movement, but its presence curdled her stomach.

Narlaw, she whispered.

Tuanne had already drawn her bow and Nara's first thought was to curse the fact that they had failed to redo the quickening of their arrows since using them in the Rift.

But it was too late to change that now. The demon had sensed them. Nara felt it turn. To her eyes it was a shadow within a shadow. To her

Whisperer sense it was a deep and terrible blight on the woodlands around it.

It came at them, darting across the meadow.

Flame bristled, ready to fight beside them.

Tuanne's bow twanged and the arrow thumped home.

The demon faltered.

Link with me! urged Nara.

She reached for the earth trance, sinking, joining with the great mass of life all around her. Tuanne's presence flowed with hers.

The demon came again, wounded but fast.

Tuanne released another arrow and again it struck home through the impenetrable dark. Again Nara was amazed at the young nomad's skill.

The demon fell then scrambled up. It was just a few dozen paces away.

Flame edged out in front of Nara and Tuanne, her claws and teeth bared ready to defend the group.

Nara reached out, channelling the earth as she had done in the Rift. She kneeled in the wet grass and gave everything – all of her power and all of

Tuanne's power, too. She felt Tuanne's warrior spirit and the bow in her hand as it once again let loose.

The earth flowed through Nara and for an instant the demon's presence was all she could feel. She swayed on her knees and heard Tuanne gasp at the incredible rush of sickness.

Then stillness came. The night returned. Nara opened her eyes and felt the cold of the grass against her skin, soaking through her clothes.

"It's gone," breathed Tuanne.

The trees shook gently in the breeze and they both stared into the black, waiting, hoping there were no more to come.

Another shape emerged from the undergrowth to their left. Nara tensed and Tuanne drew her bow.

"It's ready," hissed Olmar. "We can..." He stopped short when he noticed an arrow trained on him and a leopard ready to pounce. "Did I miss something?" he asked.

"Don't worry," said Nara, standing. "We took care of it."

Flame flicked her tail, still scanning the dark.

Olmar nodded. "We should go," he said. "Now."

They moved off quickly and soon reached the boat. Olmar pushed them away from the east bank and dipped the oars, sending them gliding out across the black surface of the water towards the fire-lit city.

Nara peered up as they approached the ruined mass of the bridge. It had been broken at the city end, perhaps to stop the Narlaw forces attacking from two directions at once. She thought how frightened the city-dwellers must be feeling, with their homes and their lives in such unexpected danger.

The river gate was set into rocks at the base of the immense city wall. The boat bumped against the rocks and Olmar used an oar to shove them along to a small inlet. A soaking length of rope hung from an iron hook that had been driven into the rock. Olmar grabbed it and moored the boat. The passengers clambered out one by one on to the slippery rocks.

Together they scanned in all directions until they were sure no Narlaw were near. Then Olmar rapped on an iron door that was indistinguishable from the weathered stone around it. A lookout hole slid open.

"Olmar?" muttered a gruff voice.

"Who else?" said Olmar, dipping his face into the dim light that spilled through the hole.

Bolts clanked and the door creaked open.

"Well, well," said a large, bearded man. "You've brought some friends?" He held the door wide. "Come on, before something sees us."

Inside the wall was a room about two paces square that contained nothing but a worn wooden chair and a single candlestick. A staircase led up into darkness and it was so narrow that Nara wondered how the broad gatekeeper had managed to get down to his post.

Olmar led them up into a winding, damp labyrinth of passages. He held a solitary candle high, casting more shadow than light across the dripping grey stone walls.

At ground level they emerged into the turmoil. Nara had thought herself exhausted from her travels, but the faces she saw now made her feel lucky in comparison. They were smoke-blackened and many looked terribly ill. The acrid smell of burned thatch was everywhere and people thundered past carrying buckets, as orders for more water were shouted above the general din.

Olmar guided them through the chaos towards a crenellated castle keep that was the tallest building in the walled city of stone. They passed makeshift hospitals and Nara glimpsed rows of sick beds, medics rushing between them by candlelight.

As they reached the doors of the keep a cry went up. "Take cover!"

Olmar grabbed the two Whisperers and shoved them through the stone archway into the keep. Flame dashed in between Nara's feet and a great boom rocked the walls of the tower. Nara turned to see a shower of fine rubble and burning embers fall into the street outside.

"Fire bombs," said Olmar with disgust. "These demons can set light to almost anything."

"It's one of their ways of feeding," Nara said.

She had been taught this as a novice, in those cosy, familiar times that now seemed worlds away.

Olmar shook his head. "Come," he said. "Lucille will be glad to see you."

They climbed a broad set of stairs, lined with burning torches. The people they passed here wore leather armour, occasionally a steel breastplate or helmet. For once, no one had the energy to stare at Flame or Nimbus.

"This is where the militia is based," said Olmar. "We have no real army in Altenheim, which is why we need help so badly. Lucille sent word with her hawk, but so far we've heard nothing in response. We don't even know if the bird made it to the capital."

His grim look suggested he did not think help was on its way.

They had reached the top of the stairs and a long hallway ran to the left and right. There were huge oak doors at intervals along the hall, most of which were guarded. Olmar asked after Lucille and a guard thumbed them towards a heavily guarded door.

The door swung open and a tall, hollow-cheeked woman appeared, a woman Nara knew well and yet barely recognized.

"Lucille!" Nara cried.

The woman stared for an instant then clasped Nara to her. "Nara! Thank the stars!"

The siege seemed to have taken its toll on Lucille – she had lost weight and her face was gaunt.

"Who are your friends?" Lucille asked.

"This is Tuanne, and this is Nimbus. They're nomads of the Red Sands tribe."

Lucille nodded gravely. "On behalf of the kingdom, I thank you both for coming," she said. "Now. We cannot waste a moment."

She thanked Olmar, who nodded to each of them before he left. Then Lucille led them deeper into the keep, up a winding staircase and into a huge, square chamber with a long veranda on one side. The room contained a bed and several large tables strewn with maps and papers. Lucille strode to the veranda, which faced west across the city to where the battle raged.

"Those woods," Lucille said. "The Narlaw command is hiding there. Can you feel them?"

Nara approached the battlements warily,

wondering how high up the tower a fire bomb could strike. Tuanne hung back with Nimbus and Flame.

The view was a grim one. Altenheim burned in several places, the brave residents scurried about and all the while the main gates were beset by the Narlaw forces. Altenheim militia barricaded the gates and shot arrows down. Nara looked further, past the wall and the battle lines to the woods beyond. Fires burned there, too. And by the light of those flames she saw movement, slow and deliberate – not like the chaotic, surging masses that attacked the city walls. This was the Narlaw camp. The true size of the demon army was hidden in the wooded hills.

"They've been weakening the city with fire," said Lucille, "testing its defences while they keep their main force out of reach. Perhaps they thought there were more Whisperers here."

"What are they waiting for?" asked Nara.

"I don't know for sure. Perhaps for reinforcements, or for the defenders to starve and give up. As things stand, the city can't survive much longer. We're virtually out of food and arrows. We can barely get enough water into the city to put out the fires. The Narlaw will attack soon, in force, and there will be no defence against them."

"What are we going to do?" asked Nara.

"We need to evacuate as many people as we can and retreat to Meridar," said Lucille. There was such exhaustion in her voice that Nara wondered if she had given up already.

"But won't help come?" said Nara. "You sent Jet, didn't you?"

"She should have returned by now. I cannot feel her presence. Perhaps because she's so many miles from me, or…"

She trailed off, but Nara knew exactly what she was thinking.

"We have boats," Lucille continued. "Not enough to take the whole city, but some will be saved at least. Our task is to engage the demons at the front gate, to give the evacuees as much time as possible."

Nara placed a hand on Lucille's arm. "There are three of us now," she said. "We'll make the plan work and get these people to safety."

Lucille smiled. "You have a good heart, Nara," she said, staring out at the chaos of Altenheim. "We'll do what we can. I only hope that is enough."

A cry went up in the streets below. "Cover!"

The fire bomb crashed against a building immediately below the keep and Nara ducked instinctively.

Lucille stood unflinching, her eyes staring blankly at the woods and the shapes that moved between the trees.

CHAPTER 14

The Narlaw attack began at dawn – when the river mists drifted into Altenheim, curling through the streets and mixing with the smoke of burned and ruined homes.

Nara had eaten some stale bread and curled up on the floor of Lucille's chambers. She was woken after just an hour or two by the terrible clamour at the gates.

They're here, said Flame, peering out towards the veranda.

Nara rose, and so did Tuanne and Nimbus. Lucille had been right – the main Narlaw force was coming.

Nara quickly gathered her bow and arrows, and together with Flame, Tuanne and Nimbus, she left the keep. There was only one way they could help defend Altenheim, and that was to fight at the front line, working together to banish every demon they could. They ran through the dawn light, passing frightened, weary faces as the sounds of battle grew louder. The air was colder than anything Nara had felt before, even with the fires burning in the rooftops. The main gates had been barricaded with every piece of timber that could be found. Fire bombs hissed overhead and rocks flew in both directions.

On the battlements, archers moved about, ducking and sending arrow after arrow into the demon army below. Nara ran to the steps built into the side of the wall, and Flame and Tuanne followed.

We must link, she whispered to Tuanne as she climbed.

Yes, replied Tuanne. Nimbus balanced on her shoulders, her lips drawn back in fright.

The two Whisperers arrived on the battlements and Flame joined them, prowling up and down, nostrils flaring and her tail straight and bushy.

Nara stepped forward and took her first look

down at the battle for the gates.

The buildings that had once crowded around the outside of the wall were now nothing but shells of broken stone. Furniture, clothes and shattered ornaments were strewn amid the rubble, and all around these ruins were hundreds upon hundreds of Narlaw.

Their grey eyes glowed and they moved with inhuman speed. Most had taken the forms of men and women, but some went as dogs, scampering like mad things between the legs of the others. The presence of their evil was overwhelming.

For a few seconds Nara stood in shock and watched them crash against the portcullis, tearing rocks from the rubble and throwing them at the walls. A short way back she saw a group of demons clutching a chunk of wood. The wood burst into flame and the demons flung it over the wall.

Nara turned to shout, "Take cover!"

Militia fighters scattered as the fire bomb struck, sending down a cascade of flames and rock dust from a nearby building.

With shaking legs, Nara stepped away from the battlements.

Are you ready? came a whisper from below.

It was Lucille.

Nara saw her down at the barricaded gates, pacing back and forth with her eyes closed.

I think so, Nara replied.

Good, said Lucille. *We must hold the demons until all of the evacuation boats are across the river.*

Nara nodded at Tuanne and then slipped into the earth trance, trying hard to withstand the ferocious presence of the demons. She reached out to Tuanne and felt her friend's presence come to meet hers. Next Lucille joined and they completed the circle – three Whisperers together, pooling and focusing their strength.

Nara felt the writhing mass of Narlaw burst upon her. She chose one, right beside the portcullis and brought its presence close. With three Whisperers at work the earth rushed through them in a powerful instant and the demon was gone.

Nara steadied herself and moved on to the next.

It was slow, difficult work under the rain of fire bombs and masonry. More than once Nara found herself kneeling, or lying flat on the walkway behind the battlements as deadly missiles flew overhead.

Flame paced anxiously. There was little she could do from the battlements but watch Nara and the others, warning them if a fire bomb was flying their way.

The sheer numbers of the demons at the gate soon took its toll. An hour after dawn the first portcullis fell. There was an ear-splitting scrape and clang as it burst free of its stone runnings. The chains that held it flew and whipped and the militia on the battlements nearby leaped away in alarm.

"More wood for the barricade!" called a senior militia woman below. "If that second portcullis goes, we're done for!"

Nara tried to put the thought out of her head, but she wondered how many of Altenheim's people would escape before the collapse of the gates.

She cast out again and again, dropping into the trance, letting the earth expel the demons one by one. But there were simply too many of them and time was running out.

Before then, all of the Narlaw's strength had been focused on the gates and the fire bombs. Now, spurred on by the fall of the first portcullis, the demons began to climb the walls. There was a shout from the battlements and Nara looked across. At the far end, away from the thick of the battle, the Narlaw had scaled the wall by climbing over each other's backs and now a grey-eyed demon was sprinting at Nara and Tuanne along the walkway.

Tuanne left the Whisperer circle and spun away, letting off an arrow in one swift movement. Nara reached out with her senses and grasped the charging demon as the arrow struck. It vanished into an ashy shadow, back to the Darklands.

"They're lifting the gates!" came a cry from below. "Secure the wheels!"

Nara spotted a demon on the battlements at the other side of the gate tower. It had thrown the defenders off the wall and unlatched the lever that locked the final portcullis shut.

"They're coming through!" shouted the commander at the gate.

Can you make it up the wall? Nara asked Flame. *We have to lock that portcullis down.*

I can try, said her companion. She dropped into the yard and disappeared.

The portcullis creaked as the Narlaw raised it higher. Nara reached out past the gate tower with her Whisperer sense and the demon swung to face her, grey eyes glaring. Nara let the earth rush through her and, a split second later, all that remained was a stain of ash on the parapet.

The gates boomed as the first of the demons slipped beneath the portcullis and charged into them. Flame was nowhere to be seen.

Then Nara saw a white-and-red shape fly from Tuanne's shoulder. Nimbus was leaping over the battlements and the gate tower almost faster than the eye could see. Before Flame had even reached the stairs, Nimbus was at the crank wheels.

Nara glanced at Tuanne, who was staring intently at her companion. Nimbus swung on an iron lever with all her weight and the wheels spun. The portcullis crashed shut, trapping the few Narlaw who had made it through to the gate. Now Nimbus twitched and darted between the mechanical parts of the crank wheels until she settled on the locking lever. She shoved it into place just as Flame arrived by her side.

You did it! said Nara. *You whispered together!*

I know, Tuanne replied. She couldn't hide her smile.

Together, the three Whisperers banished the demons that had been trapped between the portcullis and the gates. They'd bought a little more time, but not much. Beyond the walls the Narlaw army attacked with a new fury, crashing against the portcullis and the walls of the gate tower.

A cry came from below and Nara lost her connection with Lucille. She glanced down and saw her mentor lying on her side, clutching her head. She had been struck by a ricocheting piece of rock.

Go! cried Lucille. *Run!* She climbed back to her feet, but she was unsteady and her eyes were wide with terror.

Nara turned back to the battlements. The archers who had been shooting next to her were gone. A Narlaw stood in their place, glowering at Tuanne as another clambered over the wall.

Tuanne raised her bow but the demon leaped at her, knocking her from her feet and sending Nimbus rolling across the walkway with a terrible screech.

"No!" Nara cried as the demon advanced on Tuanne.

The second demon fixed Nara in its grey-eyed stare and sprung at her.

Nara stumbled sideways along the parapet, trying desperately to find the earth trance. But the demons were so close, their presences too strong for her to grasp on her own. She glanced across at Tuanne – and at the demon who was reaching out its hand to her forehead.

This could not happen. Not the ghost-sleep.

Nara had promised that she would bring Tuanne back safely.

She cast out wildly with her senses, ignoring the demon bearing down on her and trying only to banish the one who had Tuanne in its sights.

It was then a terrible snarl filled the air. Nara looked up to see Flame leap from the gate tower, a blur of savannah-gold against the dull grey stone. She landed on the neck of the first Narlaw intruder, twisting with all her weight and dragging the demon away from Tuanne. The demon fell, flailing as Flame's teeth bit deep.

Tuanne scrambled away and grabbed her bow. As Flame took down her demon prey, Tuanne's first arrow thudded into the demon advancing on Nara.

Now! cried Flame.

And Nara found her focus, slipping smoothly into the earth trance as if there was no battle raging around her at all.

In a blinding rush, both demons vanished from the earth.

Flame dropped on to the ashy shadow of the Narlaw she had been fighting. She shook her head and staring around blankly, sick and disoriented by the poisonous taste of Narlaw flesh.

Nara ran to her and took her head in her hands.

Come on, she said. *We have to go. Now!*

Flame stared back, confused, and Nara turned to Tuanne for help.

But Tuanne was at the battlements, gazing into the distance at the north road. Nara stood and looked. A plume of dust was advancing towards the city from where the road emerged between hillsides.

"What is it?" Nara asked.

"Riders," said Tuanne. "Hundreds of them."

They thundered into the valley with a flurry of bugle cries. More bugles sounded in the woods on the hilltop and a battalion of foot soldiers emerged. The Narlaw at the gates were forced to turn.

"They came," muttered Nara. "Jet must have made it through to Meridar."

It was then Nara sensed the presence of a Whisperer out there on the battleground. She scanned the lines of infantry and saw a ring of soldiers. At its centre was a fighting Whisperer. She was young, perhaps even younger than Nara, and her hair streamed in the wind. A huge, grey-black wolf loped beside her. This girl and her wolf companion advanced within the shield of warriors, banishing the demons around them as they went.

The Narlaw retreated, and Nara felt them slide away, past the walls of the city towards the untouched countryside. The two groups of soldiers joined forces and fought their way to the city gates. The troops formed a defensive line, steam rising from the horses as they stamped and snorted in the cold morning air.

Nara breathed deeply and shared a disbelieving smile with Tuanne.

By midday Altenheim was empty. Those who had not escaped across the river followed the road north under heavy guard. The soldiers' leader, a guard named Valderin, said the demons would soon regroup.

Nara was among the last to leave. She passed beneath the ruined gate tower with Lucille and Tuanne.

Although she had been offered a horse, Nara preferred to walk. Horses were not a common sight back on the endless plains and none of the girls had ever learned to ride. So the three friends joined the ranks of the soldiers on foot, marching north on tired legs with Flame prowling and Nimbus scampering behind them, side by side. Flame had not quite recovered from her taste of demon flesh and Nara kept looking back to check on her as they walked.

The girls walked in silence for a long time, each of them absorbed in their own thoughts.

Lucille at least looked happier. She had news of Jet – her companion had made it to Meridar with a badly injured wing, passing on her vital message. She was now resting at the palace. Nara couldn't imagine how it would feel to be separated from Flame for so long, not knowing if she was hurt, or lost, or worse.

Nara wondered about her parents – what would they think about their daughter fighting battles? Would the news reach them? Would they change their minds about her being a Whisperer?

But Nara knew it didn't matter what her family thought. She was among Whisperers now and she had Flame by her side. She felt peace as she marched towards Meridar, knowing this was all she would ever need.

CHAPTER 15

A high wind blew from the south. The flags on the outer walls rippled and cracked and Dawn's hair flew about her in a whirl of black. News had reached the palace that morning of the breaking of the siege at Altenheim. Most of the people had been saved from the Narlaw, but the city itself was little more than a ruin.

Dawn shifted on the bench she had taken at the edge of the palace parade ground. Her ankle still hurt to stand on, but thanks to another round of healing she could at least walk. She had made her way down from the spiral tower to keep watch for Narlaw amongst the soldiers. Still, after two days of vigilance, the demon who had invaded Ona's quarters had not been found.

Militia crowded the cobbled expanse before her. Several times each hour the gates creaked open, and wagon wheels and hooves clattered across the drawbridge. There were guards returning from leave with their families, tradespeople bearing armour, weaponry or food. Dawn cast her senses carefully, lingering on each and every presence in the yard. Overhead, Ebony was circling, scanning for Narlaw.

The preparations for war had consumed most of Dawn's waking hours, but she had managed to join Princess Ona in making an inventory of her belongings. The more Dawn had read, the more convinced she was that Queen Amina's earthstone was what the Narlaw were after. The war diaries referred to the stone as little more than a trinket, but there were other, older books that hinted at a fabled and precious artefact, a direct link to the earth and a source of great power to any Whisperer who wielded it.

Queen Amina had written of its changing colour, its small size and its setting in an ornate bronze ring that she had worn on her left forefinger.

It was possible that Amina had been unaware of the weapon she carried, even as it multiplied her power against the Narlaw. It was also possible, Dawn knew, that the earthstone had been lost in the intervening years – especially since she and the princess had failed to find anything like it in Ona's collection of rings.

Dawn continued her study of the guards and the militia, of the myriad palace servants and tradespeople who dashed or loitered or led their horses across the blustery parade ground. How could the Narlaw spy have evaded them for so long? She had placed Whisperer sentries in secret spots around Ona's wing of the palace. She had asked Magda to bring her a roster of all of the Guards of the Sun and everyone who might have somehow acquired a uniform. By now almost every member of the guards had been brought before Dawn or one of the other Whisperers. And yet the demon remained at large.

Ebony swooped down, batting her wings against the turbulent wind.

Nothing, she said. *Fled or hiding, perhaps?*

Perhaps, said Dawn. *You must be tired from flying in this weather.*

Tired, but not defeated, said Ebony. She stretched her neck, clacking her huge black beak in something like a yawn.

Ready for another night watch? asked Dawn.

The plan was that they would act as hidden sentries close to Ona's chambers. The thought of another sleepless night was enough to send a wave of tiredness through Dawn's body. But they couldn't afford to let the Narlaw get what it wanted. If she was right about the earthstone, it could be their only hope of victory over the Narlaw. She simply *had* to find it before it was too late.

Dawn thought back to the evidence from the night of the intrusion – the emptied cupboards, the clothes and jewels cast across the floor. And the guards seeing nothing, hearing nothing.

This was still the most difficult element to understand. How could those highly trained guards fail to hear an intruder ransacking the chambers they were guarding? Dawn had met each member of that night's watch and each had been as puzzled as she was, not to mention ashamed. Their logs of the night's work were meticulous. No stranger entered or even approached those doors.

No one but those guards were sighted around Ona's chambers at all, except...

Dawn rose to her feet as the thought hit her. It tumbled onwards in her mind, gathering momentum.

"No," she muttered, digging into the inner pocket of her coat for Magda's report from that night.

What is it? asked Ebony, tilting her head.

Dawn unfolded the creased sheet of paper. There were the names of the guard teams, their statements and a precise timeline written into the margins by Magda. Halfway down the page Dawn found what she was looking for:

Early, second hour of the third watch, Guard Captain Niels stood sentry at doors while Guards Humboldt and Blake attended a disturbance in the upper kitchen.

Niels was there alone, said Dawn. *He wasn't interviewed by Magda.*

But he's the Captain of the Guard of the Sun, said Ebony. *The king's personal bodyguard.*

Dawn rolled up the report and thrust it into her pocket, striding towards the palace on her aching ankle.

Ebony gripped tightly on to her shoulder, struggling to keep balance. *You're serious?* she asked.

Have you seen Niels lately? asked Dawn in response. *He hides away with the king, knowing Whisperers are barely welcome there. It has to be him.*

Ebony cawed and flapped into the air as Dawn strode on below.

Wait for me outside the King's Keep, she said. *And be ready.*

In the king's reception chamber, Lady Tremaine greeted Dawn with a curt nod. She rose from her tidy desk and the assistant hovering at her side glanced uneasily between the two of them, expecting trouble.

"You have news for the king?" the warden asked.

Dawn drew up close to the warden, at the same time reaching past her with her Whisperer sense, probing for a demon presence.

"No news, Lady Tremaine." Her voice hushed. "Is Captain Niels here?"

The warden frowned in confusion. "He is away for the moment," she said. "May I ask what your business is?"

Dawn glanced at the warden's assistant in a way that made the man bow and hurry from the room.

"I suspect the captain can tell us who the Narlaw spy is," Dawn said.

Another puzzled look followed from the warden, then one of realization. Her jaw dropped. "Surely not?" she said. "You mean…?"

"I may be wrong," said Dawn, "but we must find him at once."

The warden looked away, her face colouring. "Oh no," she said, holding a hand to her cheek. "But … he … he went to meet the princess," she said. "We arranged it with the king. Ona is being moved to safer quarters."

"Where?" Dawn demanded. "Where are they to meet?"

The warden stammered, closing her eyes as she tried to remember. "Somewhere on the east side," she said at last. "The south-east quadrangle."

Dawn turned and rushed towards the door, leaving the warden standing. "Sound the alarm!" Dawn shouted as she ran. "Niels mustn't leave the palace!"

Ebony! she called across the bond. *Fly to the south-east quad. Niels is there with Ona. Do not lose sight of them!*

On my way, said Ebony.

Dawn raced down the staircase, ignoring the terrible pain in her ankle. The south-east quadrangle was on the opposite side of the palace, far from the King's Keep and the Whisperers' quarters. There were stables there, too, and a small reinforced gate accessible only for guard patrols. Dawn cursed her own stupidity. How could she have missed this? She burst past the guards at the base of the keep, out into the violent wind.

"Follow me!" she commanded. "And one of you find Lieutenant Magda. Bring her to the south-east quadrangle!"

The guards stood, unsure for a moment, shocked to be given such orders by a young girl.

"A demon has taken the princess!" Dawn shouted.

This jerked them into life.

Dawn ran as fast as her ankle would allow, grimacing through the pain as the boots of the guards thumped all around her. They passed through the gardens around the keep, then on to the walkways of the eastern wing.

Dawn desperately tried to figure out why the Narlaw had chosen to kidnap Princess Ona. It didn't make sense. In the form of the guard captain the demon could have lured Ona away at any time it pleased. Everything came back to the earthstone. Dawn could only imagine that Ona had the earthstone on her person and that, as a last resort, the Narlaw had opted to take them both.

If this was the case, it was doubly important to stop Ona from being taken.

But as she ran behind the guards, Dawn knew that they had no chance of reaching Ona in time. Her only hope was that Ebony would.

Princess Ona walked swiftly behind Captain Niels through a quadrangle she barely remembered setting foot in before. It was so far away from her own chambers, and so drab-looking. The captain's dark cloak flapped in the wind. Fallen leaves from the flowerless border shrubs crunched beneath Ona's silver-stitched shoes. If she had known she would be walking so far, she would have worn something less pretty and more comfortable on her feet.

She peered up at the grimy windows that overlooked the quadrangle. There barely seemed to be anyone around at all. The smell of horse dung drifted on the wind and Ona screwed up her nose. She glanced behind at the second guard. He was younger than the captain and he looked almost as confused as she felt.

At the far side of the quadrangle, Captain Niels

led them beneath a low archway and into a dim cobbled yard. The smell of dung intensified and Ona reached for one of her perfumed handkerchiefs. One side of the yard was lined with stables, the other was a blank wall, and at the far end there was an open gate through which Ona could see and hear the everyday bustle of the city. In the centre of the yard stood a covered cart with a grocer's insignia painted on the side. The horse harnessed to it looked healthier than the ones who snorted and shifted nervously in the reeking stalls.

The captain continued into the yard and Ona became suddenly nervous at being so close to an open gate in the palace wall. She never left the palace without considerable planning – her father simply wouldn't allow it. The guard at the rear seemed to be having similar reservations.

"Sir," he called out. "The princess's new quarters are that way. The king said…"

Captain Niels turned, his eyes narrowing as he strode towards the guard. Ona stepped out of his way, still holding her handkerchief to her nose.

"Sir?" the young guard said.

The captain walked straight up to the other man and placed the palm of his hand on his forehead. The guard's eyes rolled back in his head and an instant later he crumpled to the floor.

Ona gasped, staring at the man now sprawled on the hay-strewn cobbles.

Captain Niels slowly turned to her. There was a change in him, a blankness that sent a chill through Ona's flesh.

She knew then, without a doubt, that this was the demon Dawn and the whole palace had been hunting.

The captain advanced on Ona and she stumbled back. She turned and began to run, but after just a few panicked strides the demon's hands clamped down on her arms. She twisted and cried out as it lifted her from the ground and carried her to the cart in one swift motion. The demon shoved her inside, her knees scraping on the rough wood planks. Ona spun and lunged for the door.

As the demon reached to slam the cart door shut

it seemed to flinch away from her. Ona stopped, wild-eyed with panic and confusion. The demon's eyes were focused on the necklace she was wearing over her dress. Ona glanced down. The central gemstone felt hot against her collar bone. Where it was normally a clear white it had darkened, clouding over like a stormy sky.

"It can't be!" she muttered.

She and Dawn had searched so hard for the earthstone. Could this really be it?

The Narlaw recovered itself and shoved Ona back into the depths of the grocer's cart. "If you scream, I'll kill you," it said.

Ona stared in horror as the door slammed shut and the weak daylight of the yard was snatched away. The cart jerked forwards and the princess grabbed at the uneven slats beneath her to keep from being knocked over. She steadied herself and touched the burning stone with her free hand.

Dawn had been right. The Narlaw really were seeking the earthstone. And now, she thought, with tears welling in her eyes – now they had it.

Dawn arrived in the yard at the tail end of the group. She saw an open gate and the city streets beyond, and a man in uniform lying flat on the ground. She panted hard, gulping in the musty sweet air of the stables.

Ebony, where are you? she called.

The reply was a distant burst of frustration through the bond. Then Dawn felt her companion draw closer. A loud caw announced her arrival.

I missed them, said Ebony. *I was too slow.* She hopped distractedly on the cobbles, twisting to look in every direction. *I need to get up there,* she said. *I need to enlist the city birds before it's too late.*

Go, said Dawn. She strode to the open gate and joined the guards who were already out there questioning passers-by and shopkeepers on the bustling street. Down the hill she could see evacuees arriving from all over the country – the city was full to bursting. She cast her senses wide and was overcome by the mass of people. She pulled back, giddy from the sensation and struck by the impossibility of finding Ona in the midst of all this chaos.

She had failed. She had let a demon walk into the palace and take the princess – and, perhaps, the one thing that could save the kingdom, too. She had felt fear before, but never this, never panic.

Dawn stumbled back to the gate and grasped the wooden frame for support. The city surged around her – voices, footsteps, the clatter of carts and the percussion of the smithies and the carpenters in their shops.

She breathed deeply and thought of her mentor, Esther, and Queen Amina.

What would they have done?

Dawn looked up and faced the world.

Panic was no good. Panic wouldn't bring Princess Ona or the earthstone back.

She strode out into the street, her pulse thumping and her mind racing. She had a new challenge to face, the most important one yet. If she failed, if Ona and the earthstone remained in Narlaw hands, then all of Meridina would be lost.

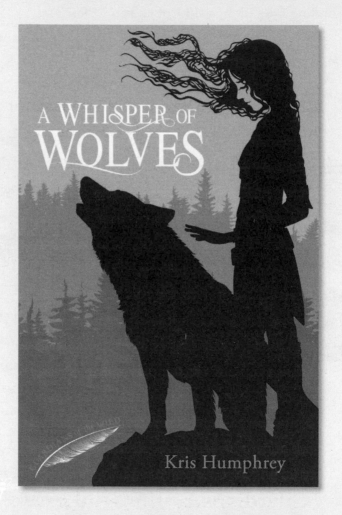

A WHISPER OF **WOLVES**

Kris Humphrey

Also available as an eBook

When a raven drops a white feather at
the doorstep on the day of your birth,
it is a symbol of your destiny. You are a
Whisperer — a guardian of the wild.

Many years have passed since the people of
Meridina last knew war, but a shadow has settled
over the kingdom. When Alice and her wolf
companion, Storm, sense a demonic presence
in the forest, they send for help to protect their
village. But they're running out of time. With the
entire balance of the natural world at stake, will
Alice and Storm have to face the demons alone?

*Read on for an extract
from the first book in the*
Guardians of the Wild *series.*

Alice hurried through the narrow streets of Catchwood. Today was market day and the village was packed with traders from all over the mountainside; boots, hooves and cart wheels rumbled across the hard-packed mud. Alice clutched a heavy wicker basket and the jars and pots within clanked together as she wove through the market-day traffic.

She stepped aside to allow a line of mules to pass and, as she did so, she noticed an elderly man sitting beside her in the doorway of a low-ceilinged cottage, carving a chunk of wood. Alice nodded at him politely as she waited, but the man simply narrowed his eyes, casting her a look of unconcealed suspicion.

Alice turned back to the street, her cheeks burning with embarrassment and anger. She should have grown used to this by now, but her visits to the village remained as uncomfortable as ever. She tried to believe what Moraine, her mentor, had told her: that although the villagers feared her now, they would come, in time, to respect her as their Whisperer. But how long would she have to wait? She was twelve years old now and had been living here, apprenticed to Moraine, since she was old enough to walk.

She stared down at her boots and the mud stains on her long, patterned skirt – the one Moraine always insisted she wore into the village. When the last of the mules had gone by, Alice left the old man to his work, wishing she were back in the forest already.

The market square was a chaos of stalls and wagons. There were so many people – and so many animals, pulling carts or tethered to the posts and fences around the edges of the square. Colourful awnings flapped in the breeze and the stallholders bellowed their prices, vying for the custom of the crowds. Above it all stood the festival tree: a solitary pine that rose up, ancient and proud. And above the tree, the autumn sky raced with clouds.

Despite the cries of the sellers, with their ferocious bustle and salesmanship, one fact could not be hidden – most of the stalls were pitifully empty. There was simply not enough food to fill the market.

It had been a hard summer on the mountain. Edible plants had grown sparse, the streams and rivers were all but empty of fish, and those who hunted rabbit and deer were forced to travel further than ever before. In fact, the village's main hunting party had set out four days ago and not yet returned. This was the first time in years that they had missed a market day and people were beginning to talk.

Alice edged through the crowd. She hefted the wicker basket and aimed for Sal's grain stall, her first call of the day. The shadow of the festival tree slid over her and with it, like an all-powerful tide, came the smells and sounds of the traders. Alice was shoved aside by people carrying huge sacks and crates; elbows jabbed at her from every angle.

It was simply the bustle of market day – she knew this – but every nudge and push made her feel even less welcome in the village than she already did.

These errands were vital to Alice's training as a healer, but Alice knew there was more to being a Whisperer than quietly producing medicines for the villagers. There had been a time when the Whisperers were respected, and even obeyed, throughout the kingdom. Under the leadership of Queen Amina they had protected Meridina from the Narlaw and banished the demon armies back to the Darklands. Nowadays any mention of the Narlaw was greeted with a condescending shake of the head. They were little more than monsters from the history books, used for scaring children into doing their chores.

Alice wished that the demons were just ancient history, but she knew better than that. The missing hunters and the changes in the forest were small things, coincidences perhaps, but Alice felt a growing fear that something sinister was behind it all – and she knew Storm and the other wolves shared her suspicions.

She felt a pang of loneliness at the thought of Storm. But she could only ever enter the village alone. The people of Catchwood didn't understand her bond with Storm, and a fully grown wolf was not a welcome guest in any village.

She arrived at the grain stall and made her way to the front. The goods on display were meagre: half a dozen loaves, a stack of wheat-flour parcels, some salt and a single coil of dry red sausage. There would normally be four or five times as much, and an extra table of wheat and barley sacks in reserve behind the stall.

Alice waited her turn, listening in as Sal finished her conversation with another customer.

"They've been gone four days now…" said the boy. He was about Alice's age, but his face was drawn with worry. He wore the short leather apron of an apprentice blacksmith or carpenter.

"Don't you fret, Owen lad," said Sal. "I'm sure they've just gone further out, looking for a better hunting ground."

"Four days, though," said Owen. "Something has

to be wrong. Dad's never been away so long before."

Sal smiled sympathetically and the boy glanced sideways at Alice as he turned to leave.

Alice met his gaze silently. Perhaps he recognized a similar, troubled expression on Alice's face because he nodded to her solemnly before he turned and vanished into the crowds.

"The usual, is it?" Sal asked cheerily.

Alice smiled and nodded, putting the frightened eyes of the apprentice boy out of her mind. She picked two jars from her basket: one ointment for the gums and one powder to help with aching of the joints – both for Sal's elderly father. Alice liked Sal and hoped she was right about the hunters – that they had simply extended their search and would return soon with a healthy stock of meat to trade. But she couldn't help agreeing with Owen.

The tension she had noticed in the village over the past few weeks was even more obvious now. The people here were forest people, just like she was. They too would sense the change in the woods – small things, hard to pin down – as well as the lack of food and the poor hunting. To Alice it seemed as if everyone knew something terrible was looming, but nobody wished to voice their fears. It made her keener than ever to return to the forest and see what news Storm had from the wolf packs.

She added two pounds of flour and a fist of salt to her basket, thanked Sal and began pushing her way out towards her next stop. The villagers barged and jostled her, casting their sidelong looks as she passed.

Once her rounds were complete, Alice wasted no time in leaving Catchwood and the market-day crowds behind. She wove quickly towards the north gate, nodding to the guard as she passed through the wall of thick wooden stakes that surrounded the village. Immediately she felt the deep relief of being back on the wild mountainside. The breeze flowed over her, lifting her hair and catching in the folds of her skirt. The musty, human smells of the village were swept away, replaced by the sweetness of the pines and the crystalline mountain air.

Alice turned uphill towards the trees and reached out with her Whisperer sense. The tree line altered minutely as a familiar grey silhouette padded into view. Alice smiled. She ran the rest of the way, swinging the basket of supplies at her side, and plunged into the forest, letting its coolness envelop her. Dogwood and sagebrush whipped harmlessly at her legs as she ran. She ducked the low sweeping branches of oaks, and dodged between the slender aspens and pines.

And then Storm was there, grey and black and golden-eyed, nuzzling into her. Alice ran her hands through the thick, soft fur behind her companion's velvety ears. The bond between them pulsed with the warmth of their friendship – and with anticipation: Storm had something to tell her.

You've heard from the wolf packs? Alice said, her words entering Storm's mind directly. She stepped back, sensing that bad news was coming.

There's a trail, said Storm. *Lifeless forest on the high ridge – scorched earth and dead trees. It leads to the mountain pass, to the Darklands.*

Alice stared blankly off into the pines. Her heart thumped in her chest.

Narlaw, she whispered.

Yes. Storm bowed her head. *We must tell Moraine. And the elders. The village is in danger.*

Alice nodded in a state of shock. Generations had passed since the Narlaw had been banished to the Darklands. They were shape-shifters, beings who lived only to destroy the natural world. Their touch had the power to wither anything that lived. It seemed so wrong to think of such things, especially here in the great forest, with the trees swaying gently and the birds trilling their midday songs overhead.

But the wolves did not lie. And they had smelled the scent of demons.

Together, Alice and Storm moved swiftly through the forest. They had no need for roads or paths. This was their home and it always had been. Even before they had met, before they had been joined by the ancient Whisperer bond, they had each spent their lives in the cool, sweet-smelling shadows of the pine trees. Alice had been chosen as a baby, when the sacred raven had dropped a white feather on the doorstep of her birth home. For Storm it had been different; animals are closer to the earth than humans and are born with the knowledge inside them. But both Alice and Storm had left their families and come to Catchwood to be trained by Moraine.

Alice often wondered about her mother and father, and she knew that Storm also thought about her own parents, sisters and brothers out there in the roaming wolf packs of the forest. Alice felt sad sometimes, not knowing about her family, but this was part of the Whisperer life, and it made her bond with Storm all the more precious. As she walked, she ran her hand over Storm's thick-furred back – a back that rose almost to her chest. It was no wonder the villagers viewed her with fear and suspicion, this young girl from the forest who walked with the wolves.

They continued through the dappled light, between hanging clusters of pine needles and the ridged bark of the trunks. The forest could give you everything you needed to live: food, shelter, water, even clothing – just as long as you took no more than you required. Greed upset the balance of the wild. As a Whisperer, this was the very first thing that Alice had been taught. And it was the reason why the recent changes in the forest – the lack of prey and plants – had to be taken very seriously.

As they approached the small hollow where their cottage lay, Moraine's voice became audible. She was speaking with a man, but Alice was not close enough to recognize his voice.

Elder Garth, Storm told her. *Perhaps they have heard of the Narlaw already.*

Perhaps, said Alice, through the bond.

William Garth was the village's chief elder. He was a shrewd man and he ran the village well, but Alice couldn't help thinking he had much too high an opinion of himself. As they entered the clearing they found Garth's horse tethered to a tree beyond the small cottage and outhouses. It shied nervously from Storm, and Alice reached out to the beast with her Whisperer sense, attempting to calm him as they passed. She could hear the deep tones of the village elder clearly now, along with Moraine's soft, thoughtful voice. She unlatched the front door and she and Storm entered the cottage, their home.

"If it's a seasonal thing then we must know when it ends…" Garth stopped mid-sentence as Alice and Storm appeared in the doorway. He was seated beside the empty fireplace and his jaw hung open for a second before he composed himself and nodded a silent greeting.

"I see you've finished at the market," said Moraine. "Elder Garth and I were discussing the worrying changes taking place in the forest." She stood in the kitchen area that was part of the large, open living space of the cottage. Behind her, on her favourite perch, sat Hazel, Moraine's tawny owl companion.

Alice shut the door behind her and nodded politely at the elder before addressing Moraine. "The wolf packs have found something," she said, glancing nervously at Storm. "Signs of Narlaw moving down from the mountain pass."

Moraine narrowed her eyes. "What signs?"

"Dead trees, lifeless earth. The pine sickness seems to originate there, too."

Moraine stared down at the stone-tiled floor in contemplation. She calmly smoothed the folds of her skirt, as she often did when thinking.

"The wolves are sure," said Alice. "The trail leads to the Darklands."

LOVED
WARNING CRY?

Visit **www.meridina.co.uk** to find out more about the world of Meridina and the tradition of the Whisperers

✴ **Read extracts from future books**

✴ **Find out which animal companion would suit you best**

✴ **Email the author**

✴ **Read in-depth character profiles, an author interview and book club discussion ideas**

Plus you'll find a range of other activities, including competitions and details of upcoming events

Follow the conversation online **#wildguardians**

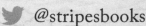 @stripesbooks

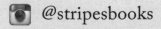 facebook/littletigerpress

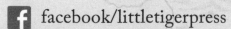 @stripesbooks

ABOUT THE AUTHOR

Kris Humphrey grew up in Plymouth,
where he spent most of his time reading books,
riding around on his bike and daydreaming
about writing a book himself. Since then,
Kris has had more jobs than he cares to think
about. He has been a cinema projectionist, a
bookseller and worked at an animal sanctuary
in the Guatemalan jungle.

A Whisper of Wolves, the first book in
the Guardians of the Wild series,
was Kris's first novel.